HOMECOMING

Celeste Castro

hoping you can see how much I love my hometown of IDAHO. It A red ass state But has beauty within!

BB
BELLA
BOOKS
2017

Bella Books, Inc.
P.O. Box 10543
Tallahassee, FL 32302

Printed in the United States of America on acid-free paper.

First Bella Books Edition 2017

Editor: Medora McDougall
Cover Designer: Judith Fellows

ISBN: 978-1-59493-555-8

About the Author

Celeste Castro grew up in Idaho and calls the Pacific Northwest home. She's worked fast-food, been a janitor, financial planner, teacher, volunteer coordinator, landscaper, fundraiser, outreach specialist, shipping clerk, delivered inner-office mail, played virgin-number-one in a college production of Camelot, been a tour guide, is an artist, stand-up comic, and worked ten years at the farmer's market (you name it she's done it with a tomato), is dyslexic, loves to travel, is a lover, and a little sister. She proudly calls herself a lifetime learner and lets those experiences drive her writing.

Acknowledgments

A note of thanks to Alexis C., Heather D., Jordan G.L., Jenny J. Hannah L., Medora MacD., Jim T. and Bella Books.

CHAPTER ONE

"You've got to be kidding me!" said Dusty. "The workshop is in Idaho? Like Idaho state?" She sat bolt upright in her agent's large leather chair, gearing up for combat.

"Yes, Dusty, like Idaho state, like Idaho famous potatoes, our neighbors to the…is there another Idaho that you want to tell me about?" Dusty saw Teggy brace herself for a duel of wits with her. It wouldn't be the first time they'd tangled. Dusty, aka Destiny del Carmen, knew she was notoriously temperamental. She was also Teggy's best-selling author, something she hoped would give her a fighting chance. "Look, I know it's probably the last place you thought you would be going, but…"

"But? No, there is no but. I am not going to Idaho for that workshop. I'll participate in any other workshop, in any other state, but not Idaho," Dusty said. "Besides I just got back from three weeks in Manhattan doing what you said would be my last talk until the summer. I need some time to myself. I haven't ridden my horses in ages. I need to start researching my next project. My barn needs a new roof."

She took a deep, calming breath and stared at the ceiling, running her hands through her long wavy black hair. "Sorry, Teggy. Not gonna happen."

"You said you would do it. They are expecting you to be the keynote speaker. Are you really going to back out?"

"That was before I knew it was in Idaho. Christ! Of all goddamn places." She groaned.

Yes, the Northwest Urban Indian Federation's annual conference was about issues important to her. But Idaho was the one place she swore she would never set foot in ever again. Even though it had been over fifteen years since she had left—was forced to leave.

"Hear me out, okay?"

"But…"

"And let me finish," said Teggy. Her voice took on an impatient edge. "This is a great opportunity for you. Your work has helped a lot of people, and it has the ability to help a whole lot more." Teggy's eyes met Dusty's. "You know as well as I do progress can only be made if the community advocates can convince the legislature to support a bill or draft a lawsuit. You being at this workshop will help add fuel to the fire that is starting in that community.

"They need to hear your story from your mouth," she continued. "These people—these families—need an extra push to jump-start the advocacy campaign. It is now or never. You want Native American families to have a chance at the justice they deserve? Give them that chance. Go to the workshop and be there for them."

Dusty closed her eyes and sighed deeply and audibly. She knew Teggy was right. Her book had helped families not only in Washington, but also in neighboring Oregon, and now Idaho was pursuing its own solution. Her presence at such workshops and gatherings helped groups give their advocacy campaigns the kick start needed to get the attention of politicians.

No, she couldn't turn her back on those who wanted to replicate her framework in their states. She couldn't say no to her agent either. She owed Teggy in more ways than one. She didn't want to let her down, she didn't want to let the families down. But she wasn't ready to face going back to her hometown.

"Look," said Teggy as she moved from behind her desk to sit next to Dusty. She took Dusty's hand in her own and met her eyes. "The workshop is only a week long."

Dusty's eyes widened and her jaw dropped. "A week?" A week was a short stay somewhere when she was on a book tour or doing research. In Idaho, it would feel like a year. Teggy continued with the same amount of caution she would take in approaching a feral cat with the intention of trimming its nails.

"It is being held in the mountains at a place called McCaw."

"You mean McCall?"

"Yeah, McCall, that's what I said."

"You said McCaw."

"No, I said—" She closed her eyes and drew a deep breath. "You're stalling and it's not working."

"It's not?"

"No," said Teggy as she retrieved the folder on her desk. "I have the papers around here somewhere. Oh yes, like I said, McCall. It looks beautiful. There are all sorts of outdoor things to do. It's being held at a resort-type place, Bear Creek Cabins, in the Payette National Forest. You won't even have to be in the city for most of the trip."

"Most of the trip?" said Dusty, eyebrows raised as she got up and moved to her agent's sixteenth-floor window. She used two fingers to lift the mini-blinds open to look out onto the South Lake Union cityscape below, unable to really see anything save the peaks of several yellow construction cranes. The buildings were obscured by the Seattle gray.

"Hold on, let me finish. Take your hiking gear and make a personal retreat out of it. Simply deliver a stunning keynote address, participate in a couple of the moderated panel discussions, and the rest of the time is yours to relax, hike, watch a sunset—hell, watch a sunrise. What do you say?" Teggy paused. "Come on, give Idaho another chance. You're an adult now, a successful writer with nothing more to prove."

Dusty sighed deeply, biting the side of her cheek. Teggy *had* kept her busy lately—had been running her into the ground. Especially after the success of *Reservations*. The book had put her on the map as a serious writer. She scarcely had time to herself anymore. And time alone was what she craved. It was why she built her home on a large piece of remote acreage well outside Seattle. Her farmhouse, nestled against thick forested land, made it easy for her to enjoy complete solitude and disappear for days at a time with her horses. But lately she hadn't been home long enough for such pleasures.

The more she thought about relaxing, the better a trip to the mountains felt. Her head had been clouded of late.

After a long and overly dramatic sigh, Dusty said, "Fine, I'll do it. I'll participate in the workshop. I'll go to Idaho, and when the last panel discussion is over, I want to come home on the very next flight back to Seattle."

"Of course, of course. You won't have to stay there a minute more. Just stick to the schedule and you'll be out of there, you have my word."

"And," Dusty said as she crossed her arms and fell back into the leather chair, "I am never going back, and I want that in my contract when it comes due." Teggy laughed, and she looked up. "I'm serious."

"Of course you are. It's a funny demand, that's all."

Dusty said nothing, because she knew more was coming.

"There is one more thing," Teggy said.

"What?" Dusty looked at the older woman, who was peering over reading glasses perched low on her nose.

"It's just a silly little favor, really, but it's important."

"What?"

"A friend from graduate school is a professor," Teggy began. "Actually, she's the chair of the Institute of Public Service at Boise State University. She singlehandedly started the department for the university. She's brilliant, driven—a real grassroots organizer there in Idaho. In fact, she helped put BSU on the map because of her service learning projects and helped bring national attention to it for something other than its blue football turf.

"Well, it was in her class that this whole thing, the Idaho advocacy campaign, was born. One of her graduate students, a Native American from the Shoshone Bannock Tribe, designed the advocacy campaign as his senior thesis. He too had watched his family and friends suffer violence without consequences on the reservation. He read your book and it lit a fire in him, in all of them, her whole class. He, along with his classmates and the professor, invested a lot of time into the campaign. They were so effective with their design they got the attention of the nonprofits and successful community advocates. In fact, they are taking the lawsuit angle, claiming that justice is a basic civil right, treaty or no treaty."

"Interesting angle," said Dusty. She tapped her finger on her lip and looked up. "Very interesting. But to be honest, I really don't feel like doing any more academic presentations on this one. The last one I did was a mess. Those kids were a hell of a lot smarter than me." She laughed, remembering all the questions they had about the tone and style of her book.

"That's not what I had in mind."

"So what do you want me to do—go to their class and give them a motivational speech or something?" She laughed again.

"Yes, exactly."

"No way. Absolutely not. I won't go into the city."

"It won't take you but two hours max and plus...you will really like her. She..." Teggy stumbled for appeasing words. "She likes outdoorsy types of things like you do."

"Really?" Dusty smirked. "Outdoorsy things? And why do I have to like her anyway?"

"She's attending the workshop in McCall too, so you won't be alone. She can bring you up to speed on all the changes you missed in Idaho." Dusty rolled her eyes.

"I know how to entertain myself." Dusty sighed dramatically. "What's her name? Is she hot?"

"Her name is Morgan West, and I am not going to humor you with how hot she may or may not be. She's an old friend of mine. You and your one-track mind. Do me a favor: Give her a show, talk to her students, and be nice to her. Can you do that?"

"Fine," she said, looking up into the air. "I'll do it. I'll meet her students, I'll do the keynote, I'll go to Idaho, and I'll be nice, but I won't like it."

"Excellent, because I already told Professor West she could count on you."

CHAPTER TWO

Dusty was not looking forward to returning to a place she hadn't seen since she was sixteen and broken almost beyond repair. She hoped to God she didn't run into anyone who might remember her. The idea made her physically sick.

She glanced out the plane's window, seeing the last of the sunset fading into purple and then black. The Cascade mountain range had long been left behind and the patchwork farmland was fading into the black below.

"Fuck it," she said and rang her call button. "I'll have another one of these"—she motioned to her tequila and ice—"and another beer while you're at it. Bring the whole bottle, if you would." Her eyes were fixed on the flight attendant's breasts. "Please."

"Sure thing." The flight attendant took the cup and purposely rubbed Dusty's fingers with her own. Dusty caught her eyes. She knew when she was being hit on. She knew her effect on women. It never failed and she rarely let an opportunity go. But this time, she didn't have the energy for it. "Is there anything else I can do for you?"

"No. The drinks are all I need right now, but thank you." Her gaze returned to the black window. Perhaps the drink would dull the pain she felt, which was still strong and fresh in her heart. Or help ease the headache she had had all day from staying out too late last night, again, and waking up too early out of the arms of Amy, or Jamie, or whatever the hell her name was. Oh, she had been lovely in bed, and Dusty would have liked to have stayed a little while longer.

Dusty had spent the past two and a half weeks mentally preparing for her return to Idaho, meaning she drank way too much, didn't eat and generally didn't take good care of herself. Women, alcohol, writing and occasionally disappearing on her horses into the mountains—they were her way of coping.

The flight attendant returned with her drinks. "Of course, the beer is complimentary and the drink is on me." She handed Dusty the plastic cup, swizzle stick and napkin that showed all of Alaska and Horizon's flight paths. She placed the beer on Dusty's tray. "Is this your first time to Boise? I haven't seen you on my flight before."

"I haven't seen you on my flights before either." It came out bitchier than she'd really meant to sound.

"Pity," the other woman said, unfazed. "I am based in Boise if you ever want a guided tour of...the downtown." She drew out each syllable. She handed a folded slip of paper to Dusty and left with a smile, eyes surveying Dusty's body. "Let me know if you want anything."

Goddamn, thought Dusty. She wasn't surprised. She had better than good luck with women. She loved them, they loved her. She would go through them for her own pleasure, wherever she toured, on whatever trip. Sex was a big part of her life, like her writing. She looked at the slip of paper in her hand. Melody was the flight attendant's name. Perhaps she would call Melody. Perhaps she would like a "guided tour" of the "downtown" tonight after all.

CHAPTER THREE

Not much looked familiar to Dusty as she drove out of the rental car lot later that night, passing more than a few parking lots dotted with the dirty dwindling remains of the piles of snow that had been scraped off them during the winter. Granted, she had spent the majority of her adolescence in neighboring Caldwell. She was awestruck at the changes as she made her way down Vista Road toward downtown. There were surprisingly few cars around. With all the new buildings in Boise, there had to have been a corresponding growth in population. Where was everybody?

She passed the Vista Pawn and Loan, rounded the bend down the hill passing the Boise Mission—she had watched fireworks from there as a child—and then zipped by Boise State University, where, to all appearances, everything was calm at the ten o'clock hour. She smiled, picturing the many drunken parties being hosted in neighboring houses at the very moment. She thought back to the kegger she had gone to her junior year of high school. She laughed to herself thinking back at how she and her friends had dominated at beer pong all night, shaming the older college students.

Before long, she was settled into her room at the historic Idanha Hotel, an old French-chateau style structure built at the turn of the twentieth century. She liked to stay in older buildings, places with sordid pasts and a ghost or two roaming the hallways. She forced herself to eat a light dinner of roasted salmon and asparagus, then fell onto her bed, her mind awhirl with memories, what-ifs and what-nows. She needed something to distract her. Or someone.

She reached into her pocket and found the slip of paper with Melody's number. "What the hell," she muttered as she flipped herself over on her stomach, fished her cell phone out of her bag and sent a text message.

I'll take u up on a tour of the city if the offer still stands?

A few minutes passed by and her phone lit up. *hh a drink, instead?*

Even better, she texted back.

The Balcony, midnight. I need to change. I'll look for u.

Perfect.

She took a quick shower and threw on a pair of well-worn dark blue jeans, a little snug but perfect for the occasion. Plus, she knew they made her ass look incredible. She chose a black V-neck, short-sleeved top—V-necks made her breasts look good—and grabbed her favorite long-sleeved flannel button-up because it was cold. She was after all a sensible lesbian. She laughed at her thought and surveyed herself in the mirror before heading out. She didn't bother with makeup. Her Latina features, olive skin, dark eyelashes and full lips, covered for her in that regard. She looked tired and she felt tired, but she looked presentable enough. She buttoned herself into her green peacoat, pulled her wavy black hair from underneath the collar and headed out to hail a cab.

CHAPTER FOUR

"Fantastic," Dusty said as she paid the cab fare, having learned from the chatty driver that the Balcony was a gay dance club.

Striding down the sidewalk, she saw food carts and people milling about. She chuckled at the familiar strip, the cars full of kids bumping down Main Street with their music blaring. She too had cruised the strip once when she was a kid, having sneaked out of the house after midnight one Friday night, friends waiting for her down the road a ways so as to not alert her parents with the headlights of their car. She had the time of her life. It was the first time she smoked a joint.

The Balcony was packed, alive with energy. Music was booming. The neon lights were shining every which way, their reflections being bounced into the atmosphere courtesy of the mirrored balls hanging from the ceiling. There were people everywhere—some dancing intimately, others on the prowl, most simply having fun.

She looked around briefly for Melody, then took the last seat left at the bar. *First things first.* She ordered her standard, tequila with extra crushed ice and a beer chaser. She took a slug of each, eager to keep her buzz going, before she looked up again—and got an eyeful of the stunning woman working behind the bar. She was tall, with long honey-blond hair pulled back in a slick ponytail.

"My goodness," Dusty whispered. She looked like someone straight out of a Hofbräuhaus. What she would pay to take a dirndl off that one, she thought, smiling at her fantasy, gently biting her lower lip as her eyes settled on the woman's full breasts and watching how the white bar towel tucked into her back pocket bounced off her nice backside when she turned to mix a drink.

The blonde was probably Dusty's age—thirty-two, thirty-four, something like that—and a lot taller than she was. And a *lot* curvier…

Someone bumped into her chair, causing her to spill her tequila down her chin a little and interrupting her train of thought. She turned toward the blonde—and saw her grinning at her as she wiped her face. Damn! She glanced at her phone—no Melody. *Good.* She snuck another look at the bartender. Her amusement seemed good-natured, at least, rather than mocking.

She was on her third drink—well, her sixth, per her habit of ordering two at a time—when she got Melody's text.

Sorry! Not going to make it tonight. Had to pick up a red-eye to Utah tonight for a favor I can't get out of. Be back tomorrow if you want that drink.

Sure, typed Dusty.

Probably for the best, she thought as she slipped the phone into a pocket of the coat resting on the seat next to her. She had lost interest and it was getting late. She wasn't here to chase women anyway. She was here for the workshop and to give a lecture in some class on Monday as a favor to Teggy.

Christ. What had she been thinking, coming here? She had to get her head straight. Which wouldn't be easy. Frankly she was freaked out about being in Boise. What if she ran into someone she knew? Or if her parents saw her here? She snorted. Her parents? In a gay bar? Not bloody likely.

But what if? Her paranoia grew with each passing moment.

Dusty's mind kicked into high gear with thoughts and emotions. Her heart began pounding and the world around her edged into darkness. She felt her anxiety building, taking control of her. "Shit." She had to get out of there before she lost it completely and had a full-on panic attack, her third in as many days. Before Teggy had sprung this trip on her, she hadn't had one in at least ten years. How would she ever make it a week in Idaho?

Struggling to control her breathing, she slapped sixty dollars down on the bar and rushed—almost ran, pawed her way—to the exit. She was about to get onto the escalator down to the street to catch a cab when the frigid air reminded her that she was missing her coat. She thought about leaving it, but her keys were in there. Her cash. Her phone.

"Damn it!" she whimpered. Taking a deep breath, she turned—and ran straight into the beautiful bartender from inside.

"Oh, sorry, are you okay? You forgot your coat," said the blonde, nodding toward the green wool coat she was holding, now the only barrier between their bodies. Her smile faded as she studied Dusty's face. "Hey, are you okay?"

On the verge of tears, Dusty nodded her head and swallowed hard. "Yeah, yeah, I'm fine," she stammered. "How about you? I hit you pretty hard. Sorry about that."

She noticed then that she was holding onto the other woman's wrist. She must have tried to catch her before she knocked her over. She didn't want to let go quite yet and didn't.

"I'll live," the blonde said, giving Dusty the sexiest smile she had ever seen.

Dusty finally let go. "It's my favorite coat," she said, raising her eyes to focus intently on the other woman's.

"Here. Let me." The blonde helped Dusty into her coat. "It looks great on you. Got everything?" She waited while Dusty checked her pockets and then… "What's your name?"

"I'm Dusty."

"Do you want to get out of here, Dusty?"

At Dusty's nod, she started toward the escalator. "Come on."

"But what about work, the club?" She eyed the bouncer who had followed the blonde.

"They'll manage," she said, giving the guy a wink and waving him back to his station.

CHAPTER FIVE

Never in a million years would Dusty have thought that she would be letting a woman she had met not ten minutes ago drive her to God knows where in Boise, Idaho.

Boise, Idaho, she repeated—no, shouted at herself—in her head. She worried briefly that everything she had done in recent weeks to mentally prepare—or avoid preparing, more like—for her trip had compromised her judgment. But had it? After all this was pretty much business as usual for her, wasn't it?

Roll with it, she said to herself. Maybe she should take the backseat for once. Let the inevitable happen. The sense of angst from earlier was being replaced by something else she could not name. Hopelessness perhaps? She felt as if she were being steered into frigid water. The resulting numbness was working its way up through her body slowly. It was not welcome.

Dusty kept her eyes glued to the window, surveying the streets, recognizing the state capitol building and the VA hospital but not much more. She thought about asking the other woman her name, but decided it wasn't important. Besides, if she had wanted to offer up that detail she would have. She wondered if she had met her match. She would soon see.

They made their way north, going to the woman's place, Dusty assumed.

"Are you new in town?"

"No."

"Oh?" said the woman, moments ticking by, getting more silence from Dusty. "I guess I haven't seen you around then?"

"No, I guess not. I'm from Caldwell."

"I see. First time to the club tonight?" she said, looking over to see Dusty nod. "You don't talk much, do you?" Her tone was gentle.

"Yes, it was my first time to the club. I was supposed to meet somebody tonight. They couldn't come after all."

"I see. Well, to be honest...I am so glad that she couldn't make it." The bartender squeezed Dusty's leg, running her hand down its length, feeling her toned muscles. Dusty squirmed and gasped slightly. She reached a little higher. Dusty opened her legs to help her.

"Can you make me feel better?" said Dusty, touching the hand between her legs, the contact giving her courage.

"Yes, I can." The blonde's voice was low and full of promise.

CHAPTER SIX

The woman pulled her car into a quaint little driveway at the end of a dead-end road. They got out and walked without further conversation toward a house surrounded by tall and budding spring trees. Dusty followed the woman through the front door, and her writer's mind immediately started noting details. Like a pile of shoes by the front door. "Should I?" She motioned to her boots.

"Would you please?" She added her own as well.

Dusty wasn't able to see much of the place before she followed the blonde down a nearby hallway, but the walls in the living room were filled with row after row of shelves, which in turn were packed with books, art, and photos. The place felt more sophisticated than she had expected of a bartender.

Arriving in what was obviously the master bedroom, she watched as the bartender rummaged around for matches to light a grouping of candles.

"Sorry." The blonde laughed unselfconsciously, "They are more for decoration. We'll have to make do with the light of the night sky." She pulled open the fabric curtains, letting the soft glow of a full moon filter into the room. She flipped on a nightlight. "What do you think?"

"Perfect." She smiled at the comment—and felt the woman's focus grow more intense. Dusty, operating on autopilot, began to reach for her, but the blonde caught her wrist, stilling her. The action caught her off guard. *Roll with it*, she told herself again as the other woman gently cupped the back of her neck, weaving her fingers into the hair there and pulling Dusty close into her.

"Off," she said, sliding Dusty's green coat from her shoulders and draping it over a chair. Her lips gently brushed Dusty's. "I want to kiss you. And then I want to take your clothes off. And then I want to feel every inch of your body with my hands and with my mouth." She ran her fingers through Dusty's soft locks and down the length of her back, making her legs buckle. She let her fall, just a little, before catching her and clasping her to her body.

The blonde took her time unbuttoning Dusty's flannel top, button by button, as if she were opening an exquisite gift wrapped in fine paper and didn't want to ruin the wrapping or ribbon. When it slid off her back, Dusty watched it float to the wood floor below, taking with it that feeling she had experienced earlier of being overwhelmed. Waiting until Dusty lifted her head up and met her eyes, the other woman pulled Dusty's V-neck shirt out of her jeans and ran her hand assertively up her stomach. At another time, she might have found the action alarming. Tonight it calmed the battle that had begun raging inside her.

"Jesus…" Unable to say more, Dusty felt herself being pushed back until she ran into a chair behind her and dropped into it. *Wow*, she thought, trying to catch her breath. This felt so strange. It was her—always her—who was in control. Who dictated the terms of her one-night stands.

Maybe it was because she was in Idaho and had been out late for so many nights prior to her trip. But this unexpected flipping of roles, wanting to be taken instead of taking, hit her like a blast of cold air on a hot day, freezing her on the spot.

She welcomed it. She had had plenty of women on her book tours. Doing *this* was nothing new. But doing this with *this* woman was. Dusty couldn't resist. Hell, she could barely function at all and didn't really want to. The sense of hopelessness that had started to consume her during the car ride was almost nonexistent now. What had felt like wading into a frigid body of water now felt like entering a warm, cozy home after frolicking in the snow for hours. The sensation enveloped her, put her at ease. She would most definitely roll with it tonight, she said to herself. As if she had any other choice!

The blonde quickly removed her own coat and her tank top. Unbuttoning her jeans, she shimmied out of them, letting them lie where they dropped. She stood before Dusty clad now in only matching neon-pink lace panties and bra. "Are you okay?" she asked.

All Dusty could manage was a nod. *Christ, what is wrong with me?* she thought as she looked the beauty up and down. "Better. Much…You caught me at a strange moment earlier. I wasn't feeling that good," she stammered.

"I'm glad. I want to make you feel good." The soft light cast by the moon through the window illuminated the woman's body revealing breasts that were full and heavy and a neck that was long and slender. She sat on Dusty's lap, straddling her. She leaned in and whispered into her ear, kissing her neck and nibbling the tender skin of her earlobe.

"Does this feel good?" Her voice was hot and wet in Dusty's ear.

"Umm-hmm." Dusty rubbed her hands up and down the silky skin of the woman's back and ran her fingers through her honey-blond hair. "So good," she moaned. The blonde leaned in for a kiss. Dusty met her lips. They were gentle and exploring at first, hesitant and questioning, then the kiss evolved into pure unharnessed passion. Their tongues battled, giving and taking, tasting and caressing, and they moaned into each other. The blonde's lips were so soft, her taste so sweet.

Breathless, Dusty pulled back to look into the bartender's eyes. The light from outside was not strong enough for her to be sure what color they were, but the feeling she got from the woman's steady gaze was that it could solve every last one of her problems.

She shifted lower in the chair and pulled the woman's hips into her, gasping as their centers met. After a beat the blonde started to move herself back and forth. Dusty ran her hands the length of the woman's legs, pressed them hard onto herself, then gently brushed her soaking center with her thumbs, eliciting an excited groan.

Dusty's hands moved to grasp the woman's hips. Her soft whimpering sent her into a dream-like state, as if she were on the last leg of an all-out sprint to a finish line she couldn't see.

She unclasped the blonde's bright pink bra, pulling it down her arms and letting it drop onto the litter of clothes below. "Touch me," the woman said, a moan of pleasure slipping out as Dusty lightly ran her fingers over her nipple, pinching it ever so slightly. It became a tight little knot in her hand. Dusty took the other nipple in her mouth, tonguing it, stopping to nibble gently. Already feeling fevered, she practically burst into flame when she felt her center being caressed slowly in response. She groaned in despair when the blonde removed her hand, then groaned again as she used it to lift the shirt from Dusty's body and to remove her bra.

"You're so beautiful, and I am sorry you were sad earlier." She kissed Dusty's breasts, licking them gently into tight peaks.

"I feel so much. So much—" Dusty said, unable to finish her sentence.

"You feel better?" She wetted her stomach with kisses, then undid the button on Dusty's jeans and zipped them down as far as she could. She leaned in to massage her breasts with the palm of her hands and then gathered them together and started licking them wildly. Dusty ran her hands through the woman's hair, relinquishing her need to control, committing to memory a multitude of new sensations.

After rubbing along the full length of Dusty's body, the woman pulled her up, led her to the bed and pushed her onto it. She removed her jeans and surveyed her. Dusty knew she had nothing to be ashamed of; thanks to the barre classes she forced herself to attend whenever she could her body was toned and flexible. The blonde seemed to approve.

"You're so sweet. Who would dare hurt you?" She peeled off Dusty's panties, then her own, and, lying down beside her, continued to massage Dusty's center. Dusty raised her hips at her touch, moaning through clenched teeth as her need for release ratcheted higher and higher.

Dusty tried to ignore the impulse that was commanding her to take control as usual, but it was no use. Letting it win, she easily lifted the woman off her body and flipped her onto her back. The other woman, taken by surprise, grew even more ravenous.

"Are you ready for me?" asked Dusty.

"Please," she whimpered, closing her eyes.

Dusty trailed kisses trailed down her body, pushing her legs apart when she came to her wet center and opening her gently. "Oh," she chuckled, feeling the slickness there. "You *are* ready for me, aren't you?" She ran her fingers up and down, taking her time, savoring the feel of the other woman before finally taking her into her mouth. She licked tenderly, tasting her and teasing her.

Feeling her respond to her, she started suckling her with tender and rapid strokes, then plunged in. The woman panted and bucked wildly. When she could feel her breathing turn into desperation and feel her begin to tighten, Dusty replaced her lapping tongue with two fingers. She slid them into her hard, getting a soft gasp in return. She brought herself back up on top of the other woman and covered her body with her own, her fingers continuing to pound into the other woman, who was meeting her thrusts with equal force. Their mouths met. Nothing held back now, they explored each other, their bodies in complete sync.

Dusty felt a long leg wedge between hers and spread her open. The other woman touched her and then slowly entered her, hesitantly, as if asking for permission. Dusty tensed up, whimpering in desperation, the instant she felt the blonde begin to enter her.

"Let go, Dusty. Let go. You're safe. No one will hurt you here."

Dusty whimpered into her neck, slowed her breathing and surrendered control, giving a gasp of pleasure as she brought herself down slowly on the other woman's hand. Meeting each other stroke for stroke, they cried out in ecstasy as they came together in a cosmic whirlwind.

Dusty drifted in and out of awareness, conscious only that she'd just undergone the most intense bout of lovemaking she had ever experienced, one that had caused time and place, Idaho and the past, to cease to exist.

CHAPTER SEVEN

"I just wish I could have gotten her number," said Morgan West. "She left before I woke up. I didn't get a chance to talk to her."

Morgan held out her palms in a hopeless gesture. She had experienced occasional one-night stands. But nothing quite like what she had experienced last night. She had commanded Dusty at first, but then had been overtaken and used to the point of pure exhaustion. But then Dusty was there, to bring her, yet again, to climax. In return, she had given the dark beauty whatever she wanted, whatever she needed.

Well, almost. The beautiful woman clearly had been utterly in need of something more. But closed off completely about it, despite Morgan's best efforts.

"I guess I'll have to settle for having the best sex I've ever had."

"The best ever? Really?" said Rosalie from behind the bar, giving Morgan a wry smile. She winked at her friend, then continued tidying up behind the bar.

"Yeah, you heard me." Morgan laughed, realizing what she was referring to. They'd had a brief stint as lovers before they decided that they made much better friends.

"Well, who knows, maybe she'll visit my fine establishment again soon and ask for another lesson from the eminent Professor West." Rosalie laughed. "And when she does, I'll text you to get your little ass down here so you can ask her for her number." She unloaded the last of the beer delivery into the bar's fridge.

"I actually never told her my name." Morgan looked down at her drink, absentmindedly tracing patterns on the condensation that had formed on the glass.

"No? Why not?"

"I don't know." She had mixed feelings about her passion-filled night. The woman had obviously been in a bad space, more in need of someone to talk to perhaps than a night of sex with some stranger. She thought back to how she had handled the woman's pain and to her own selfishness. And how she had felt waking up alone. Likely Dusty felt just as bad, though maybe not. She would never know. "It was dumb."

"Well, it's not like you do this every weekend or anything." Her friend smiled at her. "I'm happy for you. You were probably getting cobwebs down there." She laughed, waving her towel in Morgan's face.

"Shut up! Whatever."

"No, seriously. When's the last time you saw your sometimes girlfriend, whatever her name is, the woman from the BSU Art Department?"

"Oh God. Who? Alex? Nothing serious is going on there. She can't handle that my work comes first."

"You're a workaholic, Morgan."

"Perhaps." She thought back to previous brushes with love that didn't go anywhere because she didn't let them develop into more.

"You're going to need something more sooner or later."

"Oh please." She chuckled, hoping she sounded unconcerned. In reality, she knew her friend was probably right.

"If it weren't for me dragging you away from your textbooks, you wouldn't have a life."

"And thank God for that." She had spent the last ten years working on her PhD, getting tenure and building a department, accomplishing all those things years before her peers. Tending bar and dancing had been her only outlets.

"Anyway, I'm happy to see that you have that just-got-fucked sparkle in your eye."

"Oh God! I do not," Morgan protested before joining in Rosalie's laughter.

"Anyway. Didn't you say she was from Caldwell? Maybe she just came out of the closet and is starting to hit up the gay scene."

"I don't think so." Morgan remembered Dusty's expert treatment of her, the back-to-back orgasms she had given her. She seemed to know what her body wanted before she did. "But you never can know these days, can you?"

"No, no, you can't." Rosalie paused to look at her.

"It's strange because I feel like…" Morgan looked past her friend. "…like I know her from somewhere."

"What do you mean?"

"Just that—like I knew her from somewhere or from someplace. It's hard to describe."

"I hear you," said Rosalie, breaking Morgan out of her trance. "In any case, thank you again for helping out last night. I don't know what I would have done, being short a girl. You saved my ass…again," she said, pausing to dry her hands on the towel in her back pocket. "I miss tending bar with you."

"I know, me too. It was fun last night. I haven't been here in so long, what with work and all. What a crowd, huh?"

"Sure was. Hey, you want a refill?" She motioned to a glass of iced tea that now held only melting ice cubes and an inch of amber liquid.

"No, no thanks, I got to get out of here. I have so many end-of-semester preparations to get ready for tomorrow. Shit, I still have to finish grading essays." Morgan ran her hand through her hair, grinding her teeth at the thought of all she had to do.

"I have two huge meetings tomorrow, one with the Board of Regents. Gah, and I haven't yet packed for the workshop in McCall. It's going to be another all-nighter." This semester it seemed like virtually every night had been one.

She meant to get up. Instead she leaned back on her barstool, thinking about her priorities. She should have stayed in last night instead of helping at the club, but she loved the club scene, the loud music. Loved working with Rosalie. Loved burning off excess energy on the dance floor. And elsewhere. She stretched, looking to loosen up twinging stomach muscles and remembering with a smile what she'd done to strain them.

Unfortunately, there was no such thing as a free lunch. Work had to get done and now. She needed to go get ready for the last class of the semester. Which reminded her...

"Hey! Get this." She slapped her hand on the bar, startling her friend. "Guess who is going to be delivering a presentation to my Advocacy class students tomorrow? Destiny del Carmen." She heard pride and more than a hint of smugness in her tone, but it was more than justified, she told herself.

"You're kidding. The writer? Oh, I love her books! And the influence her new one has had, the true story, with the tribes."

"Yeah, that book. That was the one that really humanized her for me. I mean, I already felt like I knew her from her historical fiction, but this one... She opened her soul in it, wrote from her heart." She looked at Rosalie. "I'll be surprised if she doesn't win a Pulitzer for it."

"For sure." Rosalie nodded. "Not that I know what the criteria are for winning a—"

"God, this whole advocacy project, I am amazed at the level of energy and passion she has sparked in people. She's moved my students to try to do something about all the violence on the reservations and given them the fire they need to make change happen." Morgan shook her head. "It's mind-blowing, and I am so excited she is going to be here tomorrow. In *my* class!"

"Yeah, pretty powerful and—"

"I've spent entire semesters with my undergrads trying to get them to see that they have the power to effect change, and she does it with one book, inspiring entire communities and whole states to do something."

"You're so lucky. How did you manage to get her to visit your class?"

"Oh, I have my ways."

"Your ways and what else?"

"And I saw her name on one of the early drafts of the speakers' list for the Northwest Urban Indian Federation workshop. You know, the one I am going to next week. She's delivering the keynote address and she's going to be a panelist. I'm not sure what hope the advocacy campaign has of getting legislative or legal backing here and elsewhere, but if there's any chance, it will be a stronger one because of her inspiring presence at the workshop."

Morgan sat back, a little embarrassed by the degree to which she had been gushing about a woman she'd never met. "Anyway, when I saw she was coming, I called her agent. We go way back—had some grad school classes together—and have continued to stay in touch. So…I just called her up and asked."

Rosalie raised an eyebrow.

"Well, I had to beg a little too. She didn't think Destiny would do it. She's originally from Idaho, I guess, but she hasn't been back here for a number of years for some reason. Her agent said that she would run the idea by her anyway. Next thing I know I get an email confirming that she's on board to talk to my class. For a small honorarium, of course."

"Geez, that is crazy. Let me know what she is like. I'm dying to know what she really looks like."

"Oh, I know. There's only that one photo of her in all her books, the one where she's on a horse. You can't even really see her face with that hat on."

"I love that photo. But yeah, how she's managed to avoid social media in this day and age is beyond me."

"I know. She's almost completely buried on her own publisher's website."

"In any case, I bet she is beautiful."

"I bet you're right." Morgan stretched her legs. She had run to the bar from her house at Boise's North End after she woke up alone, ravenous, but not interested in fixing herself anything. "Probably not as luscious as Dusty was though." She gave Rosalie a pleading look. "Can't you get her number or something using the credit card she paid with last night?"

"Whatever, stalker. If you remember, she paid cash," Rosalie said. "Relax. If it's meant to be, she will come looking for you again. She thinks you work here, right?"

"Probably. We didn't really talk much, if you know what I mean." She laughed, spun around on her barstool and leapt up.

"I got to get home, grab a shower, finish grading my students' essays and get ready for the one, the only *Destiny del Carmen*," she said, drawing out the writer's name as one child would when bragging to another. "Promise you will call me if you see Dusty. The moment she steps foot in here. I'm at the workshop next week, but text me if she comes in. Or get her number for me. Or both!" She trotted toward the doors.

"You know I will, lover girl," said Rosalie. She gave Morgan a smile and a wink as she made her way out of the club.

CHAPTER EIGHT

Back at her hotel, awake after hours of restorative sleep, Dusty couldn't get over the hold the blonde woman still had over her. She blamed it on the fact that she was overly emotional and exhausted, that she wasn't herself. The woman had caught her on the verge of a panic attack, for god's sake. She wasn't going to deny it though: she did thoroughly enjoy herself. In fact, ever since she had been up she had been reliving the encounter. They had caused each other to climax over and over again, had used each other's bodies in ways that only two people in love could do.

The thought made her shiver. She had become lost in the woman's eyes, keeping her up all night despite the woman's exhaustion so she could look into them for as long as possible. Christ, she didn't even know her name. It didn't matter. Her eyes told Dusty everything she needed to know. Dusty could find her in a crowd of a million people if she had to.

Dusty lay on her bed, her laptop on her stomach. The drapes were still drawn, and the Do Not Disturb sign hung on the door. She had slept until four, exhausted, her thoughts floating between the night of sex and memories of when she had last been in Idaho. It didn't seem that long ago that she had been shipped off to boarding school halfway through her senior year of high school. One day she was a regular smartass kid, cramming for tests, skipping classes like all the others. The next, she was the new kid in "Auburn fucking Washington," as she called it at first. They had sent her away with a few belongings. And she hadn't been back since.

It wasn't because she didn't want to go home. In fact, she did. Very much so. Her parents simply didn't pick her up after graduation. She had packed up her dorm room and waited in the lobby for hours. They hadn't made contact. Instead, at sixteen, while everyone around her was excited about going to college and moving out of their parents' home, she had been wondering where she would live and what she would do next. She had tried not to be bitter at her giddy college-bound classmates. And she had mostly succeeded. She'd been more like lost and confused.

She had been lucky to have made friends with Robby Red Elk. He was her only friend at the new school. The only "out" person she had known to that point. Out and proud and eager to study fashion and move to Manhattan someday and be the first Native American fashion designer. He was tolerated but never accepted. He had been placed into the "weird kid" bucket and so was she, by virtue of being his friend, along with the acne-ridden kids and the nerds and geeks and the unathletic. He had "known" who Dusty was the moment they locked eyes in their first class.

"Hey, girl, so what do you think about Miss Turner? She's hot for a teacher, right?" Those had been the first words out of his mouth to her in their history class, knowing eyes boring into her. "Yeah, she is," replied Dusty, smiling. Grateful for that comment that first day at her new school.

She had lived with his family on the Muckleshoot Reservation after high school. The school was situated on Muckleshoot land, and his family was part of the Muckleshoot tribe. His parents had worked as custodians at the school, in addition to their full-time jobs, just so their son could attend the private and religious boarding school.

Unlike hers, his parents encouraged their son to be who he was. Dusty was always in shock and then warmed by his parents' nonchalant reaction to him when he would describe how in love he was with some favorite male movie star, like it was the most natural thing in the world. Mr. and Mrs. Red Elk didn't blink twice at the posters of Johnny Depp, Kevin Bacon and what seemed like the entire Joint Base Lewis McChord Second Stryker Brigade Combat Team plastered all over Robby's room. They accepted him for who he was, and they came into Dusty's life at exactly the right moment.

She lived with the Red Elks for three years after high school. She got a job and worked through her associate degree at the Highline Community College. She truly loved Robby's family. They had treated her with more love than her own family had ever done. But they had left her too. They were killed in a hit-and-run. Robby had been in the car too. He had survived, though not really. The pain of the loss of his parents had been too much for him. He drowned himself in alcohol. She hadn't seen him in over ten years; she had no idea where he was. All of her attempts at finding him had led to police records and dead-end last known addresses that included group homes and post office boxes across the Pacific Northwest. The accident—sadness and loss and then outrage and failed justice—had inspired her to write her latest book.

She was still surprised at the success of *Reservations Running Red*. It had taken her years and a good amount of courage to write and eventually publish it. Before, she had focused solely on historical fiction. Those had done well, but *Reservations* was different. It wasn't fiction, it was personal. It had been written to tell a story and to offer a solution. It brought attention to the violence that Native Americans experienced on the reservations, violence brought upon them from outsiders. Outsiders who were virtually untouchable thanks to a 1978 Supreme Court ruling that prevented tribes from prosecuting crimes committed by non-Native Americans. As a result, fewer people reported crimes on the reservation and acceptance of injustice was a part of their life, as was sadness and anger.

The policy framework that she had set out in *Reservations Running Red* was getting more attention—and adoption—than she had hoped for. She had hoped that people would consider it in the crafting their own solutions and use it as a roadmap for an advocacy campaign, but she had been astonished to see her language, almost word for word, in proposed initiatives in multiple states. That book had brought her back full circle, back to Idaho, the place she had been avoiding for the past fifteen years.

She had come face-to-face with those memories last night. She believed that that, coupled with the exhaustion leading up to her trip, was why she had relinquished all control with the beautiful woman from the bar. She wasn't used to letting go, but something about her had caused her to feel safe under her command and in her arms. It had taken all of her power to pull herself away and leave her that morning. She had wanted to sleep with her, wanted to wake up and feel her next to her.

It would be easy to have her again, and God knows she wanted to. Dusty knew where she worked; it's just…she'd rather not go there again. It's not like she had some silly rule—one woman, one time. She did what she wanted, when she wanted, with whoever she wanted. It just happened to be someone new every time: That's simply how it worked out.

No need to complicate things.

She opened her laptop to review her notes for Professor West's class. She decided to double-check the classroom she was supposed to go to as well as check her email while she was at it. There was something from her agent. She had been ignoring Teggy's calls all day. This must have been what she was calling about: It was a forward from Professor West.

Teggy, I am so pleased that Destiny del Carmen is able to speak to my Advocacy and Communications students tomorrow. The students put their hearts into the advocacy campaign. It will mean the world to them to have her present to them on such a personal level. I apologize, however; I will need to deviate from our original plan. I will not be able to meet with her prior to the class. As chair of the department, I have certain duties that I cannot avoid, even when there is a famous writer on campus.:) Please have Destiny come directly to my lecture hall, in the Public Affairs and Arts West Building, room 221, at 1:10 p.m. The students will be primed and ready to participate with her. After the lecture I will introduce her to my eager and excited department faculty and then, if there's time, thank her over coffee.

I appreciate you relaying this message to her, I owe you. Thanks, Tegs.

Sincerely, Morgan

"Tegs? I love it." Teggy hated being called Tegs. She followed up with Teggy: *Tegs, thank you for forwarding to me. See you in a week. DDC.*

Even better, thought Dusty. Not meeting with the professor until after her presentation would allow her to get an extra hour of much-needed sleep. Afterward, she would head back to her hotel, pack her things and get the hell out of Boise.

But first, coffee.

CHAPTER NINE

What a day from hell it had been. And it had barely started. Morgan's feet ached from walking across campus in high heels after a last-minute change of location for her meeting with the Board of Regents. Only to be told funding for her program would likely be cut in the next biennium. Nothing new. Funding public service instruction wasn't the first priority of the Republican-led legislature. She was also told again to tread lightly with her Tribal Justice for All initiative. The warning only fueled her commitment to advocate for it harder than ever. She envisioned how the rest of her year would play out: grant writing, outreach and skipping out on that little getaway Alex had suggested. Too bad.

Mondays were also her open office hours for students, and it was the beginning of finals week. The end of any semester kept her busy with writing recommendation letters. They were coveted by her students; her signature carried a lot of weight in the Boise community and beyond. Today, the stream of such students was never-ending. She was a hard and intense instructor. She expected her students to put everything they could into her classes. The students loved her for that and fought for her praise and attention. Many also loved her for her irresistible mind and, yes, her body. She had been approached many times, by both male and female students, but she never crossed any lines.

As the chair of her department, Morgan didn't have the luxury of only teaching classes. She had to attend meetings, develop budgets and manage her faculty. She missed the rhythm of back-to-back classes, the constant facilitating of learning. On the other hand, being in charge of the department gave her the opportunity to bring on more professors that specialized in public policy, nonprofits and community organizing, which, in turn, left her more time to deal with other departmental objectives.

This particular semester had been a difficult one though. One member of the faculty was on sabbatical. To minimize the impact to her budget, Morgan had decided to pick up her class. She had nearly run herself into the ground with the extra work. She vowed to commit more time to herself after the workshop, to somehow find ways to balance work and pleasure.

The Advocacy and Communications class was Morgan's baby. The class's large service-learning component demanded a lot of her time, overseeing projects and pulling strings with political power players. She had worked especially hard to convince the community organizers to work with her students on the advocacy campaign for Tribal Justice for All. Not only had she poured her own heart and soul into the project, so had every one of the class's graduate-level students. She gave them the majority of the credit. It had been their tenacity and their hard work that had driven the campaign.

She mentally reviewed her schedule for the rest of the day. After office hours, she would meet with some donors. Then she would head for the lecture hall to cover for Professor Foss, who had emailed her the night before to say that she was stuck in Chicago in a crazy April snowstorm and needed Morgan to give her students their final.

After which…she would scramble to get to her Advocacy students and her famous guest speaker. She would spend the first twenty minutes or so reviewing the essays her students had worked on. Then, after introducing Destiny del Carmen, she would give her the floor. She hoped that there would be time for her students to interact with the writer after her remarks. She was so excited to meet her! Morgan had questions for her too, though she'd be able to ask some of them after class when Destiny would meet with other members of the department. She hoped she could keep herself from acting like a giddy child meeting a famous movie star.

* * *

"Okay, students, welcome to class. After I pass out your final reflection papers for the Tribal Justice for All—excellent, excellent work, by the way—we will talk a little about how you think the actual advocacy campaign will look, from the written plan to action in the streets. Let's also talk more about what barriers you think could stand in its way and talk a little about the ever-critical public perception."

Looking at the thin gold watch on her wrist, she tapped its face. "And then, at about one ten, Destiny del Carmen will be here." She took a deep breath and paused a moment, feeling nervous though she didn't know why.

"I am so pleased with the work that each and every one of you put into this project. I hope Ms. del Carmen's presence and her personal story will help put some aspects into perspective for you as you move forward with advocating for interests that are near and dear to you. And whatever way you choose to do, be it an advocacy campaign, a legislative bill, teaching, door-belling for a cause close to your heart, writing a book…whatever you do, do it because you can."

* * *

Where the hell was she? Morgan hated it when people, famous or not, were late, and it was now seven minutes after the time Destiny Del Carmen was supposed to have arrived. God, she hoped that Tegs had forwarded Destiny her email. It would be perfect, wouldn't it, if Destiny was lost and wandering around campus looking for her? She should have arranged for someone to meet her.

Finally she heard the door at the back of the hall open. She stopped jotting down student ideas and opinions on the whiteboard and turned in relief to greet her guest speaker. That's when she saw it—that green peacoat. God damn, it was the woman from the bar, the woman she had spent hours with. This was impossible. Her name was Dusty, not Destiny.

Oh, Jesus.

* * *

Dusty was harried as she opened the door to the classroom. She had found the building, thanks to the help of some students, but had been sidetracked when she saw the students in the pottery class. She had lost track of time watching them turn pots, freaked out when she realized the time, and then gotten turned around. And now she was really late. She hated being late.

She smiled at everyone and looked around the room. She turned her attention to the front of the room, and the smile on her face froze. Jesus Christ, was that the bartender from the Balcony? Was she a student here? If she was a student, why was she writing on the board like a teacher?

Oh shit.

Her mouth went dry and her heart rate rocketed. She looked the blonde up and down, knowing full well what she looked like, *what she felt like*, under the clothes she was wearing, a sexy tailored red skirt with a thin gold belt at her waist and a cream silky gold V-neck top. Her hair was no longer wavy and in a ponytail, but styled perfectly, thick curls cascading down around her shoulders. She had long gold earrings on and sexy heels that made her already toned legs look even better.

Dusty's eyes settled on her full breasts. She had always been a breast woman, and the professor's were ideal—she knew that for a fact. God, that blouse showed them off to perfection. Dusty bit her bottom lip, trying not to show how obvious her appreciation for that blouse was. She moved to the teacher's lips and then met her eyes. She thanked her genes that her olive skin hid her blush.

Christ, what is wrong with me?

Her trance was broken by the professor clearing her throat.

"Hi and welcome, you must be…" The professor spoke slowly, as if questioning the validity of her words. Her eyebrows were furrowed. She was fingering one of her earrings, and her face was flushed.

"Destiny del Carmen. So nice to finally meet you, Professor West," Dusty said, automatically switching over to professional-speaking mode. She finished her journey to the front of the hall, marveling that she'd managed to complete it without tripping, and shook the professor's hand, feeling an electric charge pass between them as she did so.

"Thank you for the opportunity to speak to your students. I am truly honored to meet the group of individuals that were instrumental in raising awareness here of injustice on the reservations." She turned to the students. "So, I hear you all are advocating the lawsuit angle? Interesting. Though tread with caution. I mean, let's be real here, when was the last time you heard, 'Oh good, a lawyer to the rescue'?" she said with a smile.

The students and the professor laughed. That joke got them every time.

* * *

Feeling somewhat more at ease now that Dusty was addressing the students and not her, Morgan said, "Believe me, the honor is all ours. Welcome to our class."

Morgan took a seat at the back of the classroom, avoiding further eye contact with Dusty. *No, damn it!* With Destiny del Carmen. *Christ*, Dusty had said she was from Caldwell. Destiny del Carmen was from the Seattle area. Now, at least. She *had* briefly mentioned her childhood in Idaho in the book.

Despite her bewilderment, Morgan couldn't help being enthralled by Destiny's presentation. She was funny, engaging, honest and genuine. She treated the students as professionals, something that she had seen few of her guest lecturers do. What Morgan wouldn't give to have her on faculty in her program. The more she interacted with her students, the more the energy in the room grew. She answered every one of their questions, even the ones that were difficult and personal, exerting complete command over the students. *Command.* The word reminded her of their night together and how thoroughly Dusty had captivated her there as well.

Morgan's mind wandered. She couldn't help but notice Dusty's perfect backside when she turned to write something on the board. She was wearing those sexy cowboy boots again that gave her at least two inches to her petite five-foot-five stature, though she still had to stand on tiptoes to reach the top of the white board. She wore slender black slacks with yellow stitching and a cream button-up today, the soft cream color a beautiful contrast to her long black hair, which was held in a slicked back ponytail, not a hair was out of place. She looked like a telenovela movie star.

Dusty's coat, which Morgan had offered to take from her, sat folded on the desk next to Morgan. It took everything for her not to run her fingers over it. She could smell Dusty's scent on it and couldn't help but blush at the thoughts it prompted of what had transpired two nights before.

* * *

Every so often Dusty would catch Morgan looking. She got those looks from women all the time, but the look she saw in Morgan's eyes caused a burning in her chest and an ache in her stomach. She couldn't place what it was that she felt or why. She just knew that when Professor West looked at her, it made her tremble, made her come undone inside. She felt like she was a delicate piece of fabric and that Morgan was pulling at her like a loose thread.

She wanted to avoid looking at her, but she couldn't help herself. She found herself lingering for moments at a time, not quite getting enough of her. She had nearly melted when she had had to ask for Morgan's assistance in connecting her laptop into the system and Morgan had—accidently or purposely, Dusty didn't know—brushed up against her as she bent over to fiddle with the connection. Dusty nearly lost her mind.

After taking one last question and receiving hearty applause, Dusty thanked the class and Professor West. As much as she wanted to bolt, she had no choice but to stay while the professor wrapped up her lesson and said her good-byes and good lucks for the final they would be taking in the coming week. As the last of the students left the classroom, Dusty's heart beat so loudly she was certain that Professor West could hear it. She took a deep breath and prepared to deal with the consequences of Saturday's choices.

Finally alone, the two women stopped avoiding looking at each other. Their eyes met with an intensity only people who had spent hours making love could possess, knocking Dusty off-balance.

It was Morgan who broke the silence. She kept it professional. At first, at least.

"You had my students on the edge of their seats. What a fantastic presentation. Thank you."

"It was my pleasure. They are a great group. I can see why their campaign got the attention of the community. You must be proud."

"I am proud and so are they. We're honored that you came to speak to us too." Morgan shook her head slightly, looking now as if she were trying to make sense of a complicated puzzle. "Sorry, I can't—Dusty?"

At almost the same time, Dusty said, "You're Teggy's friend?"

They laughed at themselves for speaking at the same time.

"You first," said Morgan as she touched her earring. It seemed like a nervous habit.

"I am Dusty, I mean, in private. I go by Dusty in private." *Jesus, what's wrong with me?* Dusty's eyes searched the room around her, fighting the urge to either bolt or take the woman in her arms. "I mean…What a mess. I never would have…"

"Gone home with me if you knew who I was?" said Morgan, giving her a wry smile. "Me either. Probably."

"But aren't you—don't you work at the nightclub?"

"My friend owns the place. She was short a girl Saturday, so I was helping her out. I didn't have a chance to tell you that part." Both women were startled as the door to her lecture hall swung open, but the hold they had on each other's eyes didn't waver.

Finally breaking away, Morgan continued, "Destiny, let me introduce you to my colleague, Professor White." She motioned to the middle-aged man in a plaid shirt and khakis who was approaching them, hand extended. "He teaches our budgeting and economics classes. Professor White, this is Destiny del Carmen."

"It is a pleasure and an honor to have you here on our campus," he said. "When our department heard that you were coming, well, we weren't at all surprised. Professor West always lines up the best guest speakers. She can be quite effective."

Dusty raised her eyebrows and nodded knowingly at the professor. "Agreed." She saw a faint rise in the color in Morgan's cheeks. She loved the effect she was having on Morgan. And the fact that her olive skin would conceal her own blushes.

"Well," said Morgan. "Let me introduce you to the rest of my department colleagues. They are looking forward to meeting you. Can you still meet for coffee after?"

"I should really get up to McCall for the workshop. I need to prepare a few slides for the keynote. I can't drive very well at night." It was one of her more lame excuses.

"Oh, of course, sure. You probably have a lot to do before your presentation," said Morgan, a slight look of disappointment in her eyes.

"I'd love to meet your department colleagues first, though," offered Dusty. Judging from the way Professor White's eyes were shifting between the two of them the awkwardness they were experiencing must be fairly evident. She smiled, trying to ease it.

"Wonderful, right this way."

"May I have my coat, please?" said Dusty, noting that Morgan was walking out of the classroom with it in hand.

"Oh," she chuckled nervously. "Yes, sorry, here you go. I would hate to take this from you."

"Thanks," said Dusty, remembering all to well what happened the last time she had left that coat behind. From the set of Morgan's jaw, she did too.

CHAPTER TEN

"Well, did you give her a show?"

"What? Did I do what?" Dusty was surprised at her agent's choice of words.

"The lecture, how did the lecture go? You hanging in there?"

"Oh. Fine. It was fine. They were a great group of students. Why?"

"Why nothing. I only called to see how things went. So what did you think of Professor West?"

"She was nice."

"Nice? Um, okay."

"She is a lot younger than you. I was expecting someone…"

"More my age?"

"Yeah, you said she was your old friend."

"Gee, thanks," she said, laughing at what Dusty had said. "And I said she was *an* old friend of mine, not my old friend. You know that I got my graduate degree later than most. So," she continued, "will you two be hanging out together at the workshop in McCall? Do you have a lot in common with her?"

Yeah, we have Saturday night in common.

"Yeah, she's an inspiration. Listen, I really should hang up. I am getting deeper in the woods and need to concentrate. Will probably lose the connection any minute now."

She was lying. She wasn't anywhere near wooded areas. In fact, she was still in her hotel room, having retreated there after spending an agonizing amount of time meeting Morgan's colleagues. It wouldn't have been so bad, perhaps, if she had been able to stop staring at Morgan's backside in that tailored red skirt and heels and remembering all too well what she had felt like, what her skin felt like in her mouth and in her hands. She hoped she hadn't come off as uninterested to the faculty. She had been very interested—just not in what they were saying.

"Okay, okay, one more little thing. You will need to get an updated speakers' packet at the lodge tonight. They had to rework one of the panel discussion times to accommodate some hotshot legislator's schedule or something. So don't forget to pick it up, okay?"

"Can't you email it to me?"

"Pick it up, Dusty. It'll take you two minutes. And besides, I don't have it yet. I just got off the phone with the organizer. It's still being edited."

"I can wait until you get it."

"Dusty…"

"Fine. Okay. It's getting more and more green here, lots of trees. Gotta go."

"All right, all right. I just wanted to make sure you were doing okay, that Idaho hasn't swallowed you whole."

"I am fine." Dusty laughed. "Don't worry about me. Hang up."

"Okay, okay. You be good, Dusty."

"Of course."

CHAPTER ELEVEN

Dusty left downtown Boise as late as she could possibly risk it, not wanting to drive in complete darkness through the mountains. Her intent was to check in as late as possible and avoid running into Morgan. While the roads were bare of snow in the city, the mountains were another story. Snow still lingered on the roadsides and partially covered the road leading to the lodge. The road was barely wide enough for two cars—there was little room for error. She had waited too long. It was dark already and she really couldn't see worth a damn at nighttime. God help her if something did happen; she couldn't get a signal on her cell to call for help.

The abundance of evergreen trees that started to appear reminded her of Washington. She had hated everything about Washington until the Red Elk family took her in and taught her to find peace in the land around her. When she had first arrived at Auburn, the evergreens were all she could see and smell. She had hated the smell until she learned that they were cedar trees. The cedar was the most important tree to the Red Elks' tribe and was known for its healing and herbal qualities. She grew to love the evergreens then and saw them in a different light. Soon, she grew to love and crave the Northwest as well, especially when she was away for extended periods.

While the constant Seattle gray caused most people to get stir-crazy and feel like they were trapped in a bubble of gloom, she didn't mind. Especially when it misted. It was "fine Indian weather," as the Red Elks used to say. She loved the steel blue of the clouds in the sky, especially when they were low, and how the gray would sometimes settle inches above the horizon, with only a thin line of silver sun peeking out. She felt like she was in a real live snow globe, as if at any moment someone could simply lift the cap up and light would magically appear.

She sighed, remembering the Red Elks, how they would spend practically every summer evening outside, barbecuing and relaxing and watching the sky and the sun going down forever into the night. Robby was there, drawing in his sketch pad; she was there, writing in her journal. The only thing they loved more was riding horses. They had taught her how to ride, and she even had her own horse and her own saddle, given to her on her eighteenth birthday. They often spent weeks at a time with their horses, high in the mountains. She had finally felt like she had reached peace. It nearly killed her to lose them to a drunk driver. He killed them and had never paid for what he had done. He was never prosecuted and wouldn't ever face justice, not unless the laws could be changed. And that's why she was here.

Dusty parked, turned off the engine and leaned her head back, hands still gripping the wheel. There probably was no avoiding Morgan, but she would try. In Seattle or wherever she happened to be at the time, she ran into former flings all the time. Her strategy was to be such an ass that they'd leave her alone. She pretended not to know them or asked if they were into threesomes or something. It always worked.

But she couldn't stop thinking about the professor. She didn't want *her* to leave her alone. There was something about Morgan that stirred her in a way she had never felt. The thought frightened her. It had to be the circumstances: the surroundings, the emotions, being exhausted. She had simply used her for sex, like all the others, that was no different.

But she had used her for something else too. She had been panicked that night, and she had used Morgan to bury her emotions, to mask the pain. She had been obvious about it too. At one point she had let Morgan hold her, only briefly, when tears had begun welling in her eyes again and she couldn't breathe. The tender moment was short-lived; she had quickly turned her pain into unbridled passion. Morgan was able to keep up, but just barely.

Dusty had tried to hold back, but in her emotional state she gave more of herself to Morgan than she would have liked. She hadn't been planning on ever seeing her again, for Christ's sake!

She didn't want to be too rude; Morgan was Teggy's friend and she wouldn't do that to Teggy. She would simply get through the workshop as best as she could, get on the next plane to Seattle and that would be that.

Her eyes popped open as she heard another car door slamming. "Jesus." She had fallen asleep. Twenty-five minutes had passed by since she had turned her car off. Gathering her belongings, she headed for the lodge.

CHAPTER TWELVE

"Hi, I'm Destiny del Carmen. I need to pick up a revised speakers' packet for the workshop please," she said in a hurried tone.

"Destiny, oh, it is such an honor to have you here," said the woman at the registration table. "Can I just say that your story about the Red Elks, *Reservations Running Red*, was just so inspirational. It has given a lot of us hope. We haven't had hope in a long time." She clasped her hands together. "Oh, we're so excited to have you here. The advocacy campaign has a really good chance to raise awareness. Having you here has got a lot of people excited. We were so glad when they confirmed you as a speaker."

The woman's genuine, heartfelt tone caused Dusty to slow down and take a deep breath, reminding herself that she was here because of—and for—her and others like her. She was used to people gawking over her on her trips, but this woman was different: This was the first time she heard that she had given someone hope. She smiled. "I am glad that there is hope again. That was all I wanted to do with my book."

"If you need anything while you are here, please don't hesitate to ask." She handed Dusty the revised packet. As she took it, she noticed that Morgan West's was among the name tags that hadn't been claimed. Morgan hadn't arrived yet.

"I won't at all."

"I snuck a handful of extra drink tickets for the opening dinner tomorrow night into your packet, plus some coffee tickets for the little café." Her smile caused Dusty to relax a little.

"Thank you. That was very sweet," said Dusty, shoving them into her pocket. She started to walk off but paused, noting a bit of hesitation in the woman.

"And, um…" The woman looked down, fidgeting with her pen, then straightening a stack of already straightened papers on the table. "Would you sign my copy of one of your books?"

"Of course I will sign your book."

"Great! Oh gosh, thank you. I have been working the check-in table the entire shift so I wouldn't miss you," she said with a gleaming smile, her eyes bright and eager. Dusty expected to see her recent book, *Reservations*, with its simple red cover. Instead, she brought out one of Dusty's earlier novels for her to sign. Which she did.

"Oh, thank you so much," she said as she brought the book close to her chest. "Thank you again. Good night, Destiny. See you tomorrow."

Dusty's cabin was one of the few singles. The majority of the cabins were either duplexes or quadplexes. Though far apart from each other, they were arranged in small clusters. Privacy would be difficult.

"Damn it," whispered Dusty as she started to unpack her laptop and belongings. She had left her laptop power cord in the car. It must have fallen out of her bag when she almost hit that deer. At least she hoped that was the case and that she hadn't left it back at the hotel. She had driven back to her hotel from the university like a Nazgul in search of the One Ring and packed in haste.

"Well, I can't get much done without that cord," she said as she grabbed her room key and coat. As she locked her door and spun to head for her car, she came face-to-face with Morgan.

"Shit," she said under her breath, though her comment had not been not as quiet as she hoped judging by the look Morgan shot her. She thought about heading straight back into her room and almost did.

"Well," said Morgan, clearly astonished. "It's nice to see you again." She gave Dusty a curt smile. It was nothing like the warm smile Dusty had come to crave, but at least it was a smile.

"Oh, hi! You're here? I mean, is that your cabin?" Dusty awkwardly motioned to the cabin directly across from her own. She knew the answer already, as the professor had just walked out of it and was locking the door behind her.

"Yeah, yeah, it is. Is that yours?" Morgan said, her tone thick with sarcasm, her eyes focused intently on Dusty.

"Yep." Dusty knew that look. It was the look a lot of women gave her when she ran into them after disappearing on them the morning after sex. It was a look that bordered on anger, yet there was something else behind these particular eyes. She didn't blame Morgan, just as she didn't blame any of the women she slept with. She had used them and then left, ignored, avoided them. She had to get away.

"Well, thanks again for the tour of your department earlier. I left my laptop power cord in my car, darn it—can't get much done without that. Well, see you." She pulled her black knit cap down over her ears, trotting away from Morgan.

"Unbelievable," said Morgan, not quite under her breath.

"What?"

"I said, 'Unbelievable.' You are unbelievable," she said, trying to keep up.

"What? Why?"

"Well, you're so obvious in your attempt to avoid me. It's funny."

"What? I'm not avoiding you," said Dusty. But she knew she was caught.

"Yeah, you are," said Morgan, matter-of-factly.

"Look, I am sorry, okay? I wouldn't have gone home with you if I had known who you were. I don't want to complicate things."

"Oh, I see," Morgan said in a false, methodical tone, talking slowly. "You don't want to complicate things. Well, that is exactly what you are doing. I mean, we're both adults here. I get why you left, you are entitled to do whatever you want. Honestly— you don't have to avoid me and you don't have to act like an ass about it either."

She almost bumped into Dusty, who had stopped dead in her tracks. She turned. Dusty gave her a good look. Those soft golden eyes made her melt, and the long blonde hair cascading down and around her neck made Dusty want to run her fingers through it. Morgan no longer wore the form-fitting skirt and blouse that had made her breasts look delectable nor the black pumps that made her legs and backside look so delicious. Instead, she wore sexy blue jeans, a white V-neck blouse and a black leather motorcycle jacket. She still looked absolutely stunning. Dusty wanted her...wanted her bad.

"It's not like that, really," Dusty said. She started to reach out toward the other woman, then stopped. "I was caught off guard today. It's been a long couple of weeks. It's been difficult for me to come back... Teggy had to practically twist my arm to do the keynote and the presentation today," she said, immediately regretting the words. She cursed herself for already saying too much. "Shit." She ran her hand through her hair. "That's not what I meant."

"Twist your arm? Really, you didn't want to come here to speak to people who you have given so much hope to?"

"No, no, it's not like that. What I meant was..."

"What, was it a favor to Teggy and did she bribe you to speak to my students too? I bet that was the icing on the cake, wasn't it?" She shook her head and walked away.

This time it was Dusty who was trying to keep up with a trotting Morgan. "No, wait, stop. It's not like that. I do care, deeply, about the people here and your students too. Without them, none of this would have happened."

"Yeah, you're right," replied Morgan, giving up. She took a deep breath. "It's okay, I get it." She continued to walk away.

"Wait, that was my fam—" Dusty stopped, closed her eyes. "I lost my friends on that reservation. It's...I haven't been back to Idaho in quite a while, almost fifteen years. I'm a little"—*sad, weak, broken*—"tired. You were the last person I was expecting when I walked into that classroom."

"Well, I was caught just as off guard as you were. You were the last person I was expecting to see too. But you know what?" She gave her another curt smile. "It's okay. You can spare me the details. You don't have to avoid me, okay? We're going to be here for a week. The workshop will be a lot more tolerable for you if you don't have to worry about avoiding me."

Dusty said nothing.

"Okay, then, well, good night, Destiny."

Dusty felt horrible. It was an odd feeling. Usually she made women feel bad, not the other way around. "You're right," she yelled at Morgan, drawing looks from others around the cabins. "You're right. I'm being a complete ass and I'm sorry." She wanted to take Morgan in her arms, pull her into her cabin, and make love to her and ask her to make her feel safe again. But she couldn't.

Dusty reached into her pockets, feeling her café tickets. "Morgan, would you like to have that coffee after all, at the lodge, my treat?"

"Would I like to have coffee with you? I don't think so. Probably not a good idea, but thank you anyway." Morgan continued her retreat.

"Wait, come on, please? Let me get you something warm: a sorry-I'm-a-complete-ass apology coffee. Besides—come to think of it—you owe me for speaking to your students today."

"Really? I owe you?" Morgan laughed. "You really are unbelievable, aren't you?" She sighed. "Fine, just a coffee."

"Of course, just a coffee."

CHAPTER THIRTEEN

"Good thing you have all those coffee tickets. You can use them to buy me another apology drink tomorrow. God knows you'll probably piss me off again between now and then," Morgan said with a smile as they found a quiet table in one corner of the lodge.

Dusty noticed the large vinyl pop-up banners advertising the workshop and promoting Destiny del Carmen as the keynote speaker.

"Do you ever get used to seeing your name up there like that?" Morgan said.

"Not really." Dusty was quite modest about her book dealings. But she felt eyes glancing her way, felt people whispering. They were smiling at her. The check-in woman must have tipped others off, since she only included one obscure picture of herself in her books. To the dismay of Teggy and her publisher, she completely detested social media or anything that could go viral for that matter and demanded people respect her need for privacy where she agreed to speak or interview.

"So, it's been fifteen years since you've been back here? I bet things look a little different to you, don't they?"

"Yes, they do. I hardly recognized anything, not even the airport. I almost got lost on my way to my hotel, if you can believe that."

"Yeah, I can. There has been quite a bit of growth here and it only happened recently, within the last ten years or so. When Boise got its big theater, then Edwards, Nampa and Caldwell needed their own, and all the growth started. Now they have all the chain stores Boise has."

"That's funny. Believe it or not, I remember when Nampa got its first Taco Bell. That was a big deal." She took the warm mug into her hands to take a sip. "I bet this place—these cabins—haven't changed much. The mountains are always the last places to get hit."

"True. I can tell you firsthand. I spent a lot of spring and summer breaks here with my family when I was a kid. I came up here for three weeks every summer all the way through college. Everything pretty much looks the same."

"Through college too?"

"Yeah," Morgan chuckled. "A lot of my friends would give me such a hard time for bailing on them to trips to Las Vegas or New Orleans for spring breaks. To be honest, all I could look forward to was camping here with my family."

Dusty thought of her college breaks, which had been largely spent drinking and partying with girls whose names she didn't know. "Did your family camp any place in particular?"

"Yeah, we own a cabin not far from here. Well, Uncle Mike owns a cabin not far from here, about seven miles north." She pointed. "It's a fantastic hike. I am thinking of taking a little visit between meetings. You know, to make sure everything is okay up there."

"Do you still get up here? Do you still hike and camp a lot?"

"Yes, as a matter of fact I do. Not as much as I would like. I am so busy with everything else these days. But I love these mountains. They help ground me when I start to feel overwhelmed with everything," Morgan said in between sips of coffee. "To be honest, this workshop couldn't have come at a better time. I am desperately in need of some grounding." She told Dusty about her semester of teaching, picking up extra classes, the advocacy campaign and the countless balancing acts she had to do as chair of her department.

"When I was little and we'd be up here camping, I would sometimes get up really early, before my parents. My sister and I would hike on a cool trail we found. We had our own private lookout where we would sit and watch the sunrise. God, it is a gorgeous view." Morgan blew on her cup of coffee and smiled. "All I have to do is hike there, watch the sunrise and somehow things are better, body and soul."

"That must be nice, having such a simple way to regenerate yourself. I wish it was that easy for me." Dusty let her shoulders relax a little into her chair. She had thought that having coffee with Morgan would be extremely awkward, but so far she was enjoying herself. However, she couldn't help but watch Morgan's lips as she blew at her coffee to cool it down. They were driving her nuts.

"Why can't it be that easy for you?"

"I don't know. I don't think that something that simple would do it for me. I actually can't remember the last time I watched—actually watched—the sunrise." Dusty chuckled. "Let alone gleaned any of its rejuvenating properties." She actually had seen the sun rise on a number of occasions on her way home from having spent the night with her sexual partners. Of course, taking in a sunrise versus happening to catch it while driving home was much different.

"I see," Morgan responded, licking her lips. "Well," she said, breaking Dusty's focus, "I am going to head out early tomorrow morning to see the sun rise. The lookout spot isn't that far from here. It is an easy hike, a good five miles. You want to come and see the sunrise, give it another chance to relax your soul?"

"Hike with you?"

"No, I'll hike first, then you can hike after, and we will meet halfway."

Dusty was about to ask her to clarify, when she realized that Morgan was teasing her.

"Oh," she said, smiling.

"Just tell me you brought something other than those cowboy boots," Morgan said.

"I did, but what's wrong with my boots?"

"Nothing, they look great on you," Morgan said, blushing. "But they're not the best for hiking. So you're more than welcome to come with me tomorrow to see the sunrise. That is, if you enjoy hiking, brought the right gear and don't mind early mornings."

Dusty thought about the last early morning she had experienced, the one she'd spent in Morgan's arms. "I love hiking and I was planning on taking a look around during my time here. Of course, I haven't done much exploring in the mountains without my horses. It would be nice to have a, you know, a guide, advice from an expert," she bumbled. *Jesus, that was a stupid thing to say.* What was it about this woman that had made her so tongue-tied?

"Horses, wow. You actually ride? That's cool. So those boots aren't merely a fashion statement?"

"Well, they are and they aren't," Dusty said with a smile.

"Okay. Well, if you are in, I'll knock on your door at four to get you."

"Four?" said Dusty, nearly choking on her drink.

"Yeah, well, we got to make it up there before the sun actually rises."

"Oh, okay. But what about light?"

"Do you have a flashlight?"

"I think so."

"I got an extra one you can use."

"Do you?"

"Yes. Now are you in or are you out?"

"I'm in. Four thirty. I'll be up."

"I said four."

"Four fifteen?"

"Fine." She gave Dusty a stern look. "Are you sure? Last chance to bail. Because I'll knock on your door and break in to get you if I have to."

"Would you really?"

"Only time will tell," she said with a smile.

"Okay."

"Pack snacks in case you get hungry. And water. After the sunrise, I know of a great little summit point not too much farther than the lookout spot that is worth the extra trek."

"That sounds fun," said Dusty, genuinely meaning it.

"Then it's a date," said Morgan. Noting the concern in Dusty's eyes, she laughed. "That's not what I meant."

"I know."

Morgan stood up abruptly. It was her turn to leave Dusty alone. "Well, I am off to bed. I am plain beat from"—her cheeks flushed again—"from everything. It was the last day of the semester today. There was so much to do before coming here. I'm so looking forward to taking a hot shower and crawling into bed."

What a visual, thought Dusty as she stood up. "Thank you for having coffee with me," she said with a smile.

"Thank you for buying. See you tomorrow, okay?"

"It's a date," she said with a smile as she watched Morgan leave. She wondered what she was thinking.

* * *

Morgan sighed deeply when she closed the door to her cabin. "God help me," she said to herself. There was something about that woman that she couldn't resist or explain, something that extended beyond her fascination with her being a famous writer. She made her way to her bathroom and pulled her hair into a ponytail so she could brush her teeth and wash her face and get ready for a much-needed hot shower. *Maybe a cold one would be more appropriate...*

She thought how much better her shower would be if Dusty were with her. She shook her head. The woman had only wanted one night with her. She had made that very clear. But Morgan couldn't help but wonder why Dusty hadn't been back to Idaho in over fifteen years. What had happened? It was probably none of her business.

She got into the shower, moaning at the feeling of hot water on her back. She wondered why Dusty had left so abruptly that morning. She guessed it wasn't really that strange. A woman was entitled to walk away from a one-night stand with no questions asked. It wasn't the first time that had happened to her in her lifetime. But, Christ, to be purposely avoided.

Thinking back on it, though, maybe it wasn't really that strange after all. Dusty was likely embarrassed. She had nearly fallen apart multiple times during their night together and the more Morgan had tried to connect the more closed off she became, and so she did what she could, taking care of her through her kisses and touches.

She wondered what would have happened if she had told her her name, if they would have stopped. If they would have talked. She doubted it. They had used each other's bodies with such intensity, neither one letting the other rest, not for a second. Since she didn't expect to see her again anytime soon, she didn't think about the implications of not introducing herself. Likely that's what Dusty had thought too...

She had never had such mind-blowing sex. She thought about Alex, her on-again and now off-again, nothing-serious acquaintance from the Art Department. They got along, they didn't fight, they had decent sex, but it was nothing like what she had experienced with Dusty. She wondered if she could go back to Alex after what she had experienced with her. True, a relationship wasn't all about the sex, but now she knew what her body was capable of. Would she be able to accept anything less now? She highly doubted it. God, she was way out of control that night.

Jesus. What would Rosalie say when she heard that the woman she'd spent all those breathtaking hours with on Saturday was none other than someone she admired so much as a writer? She was eager for their hike tomorrow. It didn't promise to be *quite* as stimulating, but she was interested in Dusty's story. What had inspired her latest book. She wanted to find out so much more.

CHAPTER FOURTEEN

Dusty woke at three o'clock. She really hadn't slept. She kept thinking about Morgan, about how in just a few hours she would be hiking with her to view the sunrise. She made coffee and dressed in several layers. Though it was approaching mid-April, it was still close to freezing in the mountains and much more so in the wee hours of the morning. She stuffed gloves in each of her coat pockets, then loaded her backpack with two large water bottles and a host of snacks: dried fruit, granola bars and trail mixes. She thought about bringing her phone but thought better of it. Might as well leave it; she couldn't get a signal up here anyway. She didn't want to bother with it if she didn't have to.

The soft knocking of her cabin door startled her. She almost dropped her cup of coffee. "Christ."

"Hi," said Morgan, giving Dusty that smile she craved.

"Hi, come on in."

"Did you sleep well?"

"Yes, like a baby," Dusty lied. "I had a hard time waking up. You?"

"Yeah, like a baby," Morgan said as she looked around. "Wow, nice place. It's nicer than mine, and bigger."

"I don't know why Teggy books such large rooms for me. It's just me, for crying out loud." But she knew her agent always booked the best accommodations. Teggy knew her story of being sent away, of not ever really having a place of her own.

Dusty saw Morgan glance at her perfectly made bed. She thought how much better the day would be spent with Morgan in that very bed versus on the trail at this ungodly hour. She was coming close to voicing the alternative when Morgan brought her back to reality.

"Ready to go?"

"Totally."

* * *

Though they had only been on the trail for little more than an hour, Dusty was finding it hard to keep up with Morgan's pace. She was still wasted from the emotional vortex she was in, not to mention contending with being in the mountains and at a higher altitude. It didn't seem like they were following any sort of trail either. Morgan seemed to be leading them straight up the damn face of the mountain. That and the headlamp Morgan had let her borrow didn't fit that well. It kept slipping down over her eyes. When she tried to adjust it, she had looked directly into the bright light, momentarily blinding herself. The one time it had actually shone her something besides her feet and Morgan's butt, she had seen switchback after switchback after switchback ahead of them. Only a crazy person would attempt to hike this type of trail at o-dark-thirty! At least her hiking boots would be getting worked in. She stomped off a nice thick layer of mud from her boots. Again. Regardless she did her best to keep up, not wanting to have to look at Morgan's enticing backside any more than absolutely necessary.

God, she would love to get her hands on Morgan once more. But she knew better. That could never happen again.

"So, your family camps here a lot?" Dusty puffed, trying to keep her thoughts focused on the present.

"Yep, every spring and summer since I was a little girl, whatever excuse we could find to get out of Boise. I had so much fun here with my family. My dad would take us fishing. We would hike, we would read, would play games, go swimming… we practically lived on hot dogs and roasted marshmallows. Some of my best memories are of things we did up here. Then there's my uncle's cabin—or the 'bunker,' as he calls it."

"The 'bunker'?" said Dusty, trying not to sound like a steam engine laboring to get up a hill.

"Yeah, he is one of those quintessential Idaho doomsday types that you always hear about, the ones from California that come here to hide from—whatever it is they're hiding from." Morgan laughed. "He said when the end of the world comes, his cabin—his bunker—is where he is going to hide. It's always locked, stocked and guns cocked, he would say. You name it, he has it in that cabin: food, alcohol, guns, tools. He even has a shortwave radio."

"That's neat," said Dusty, trying to sound engaged and yet continue to somehow breathe.

Morgan laughed again. "He would get so mad at me and my sister when we got older. We would always get into his bunker and sneak swigs of his prized Johnny Walker. Hey, we should break in and get that! Trust me, it'd be worth your time. It is good stuff!"

"Yeah, sure, let's do it," said Dusty, wincing at the throbbing in her legs, not sure what she just had agreed to.

They continued in silence for a little ways before Morgan spoke. "So. Caldwell, huh? What was that like growing up?"

"Oh, nothing spectacular," said Dusty. "Caldwell is the land of opportunity. That's the city's motto, did you know that?" She wanted to steer the conversation away from anything personal.

"No, I did not. You do a lot of horseback riding, right? Oh, Jesus, were you ever a rodeo queen at the Caldwell Night Rodeo?" Morgan snorted.

"Ha! No! I was never a rodeo queen." Dusty shook her head at the thought. "I didn't even start riding until…"*After I was kicked out of my parents' home.* "Until later, after high school. I ride quite a bit now. I have two horses, Patty and Selma. They are quarter horses."

"So, you have half a horse?" joked Morgan. "Half a horse, get it?" She looked back at Dusty, who had stopped walking. Her confusion must have shown on her face. "It was a joke, you know a quarter and a quarter…"

"Yeah, it was funny, I guess," she said, shaking her head.

"But a quarter horse is the best horse for barrel racing, is it not?"

"True."

"And the preferred horse for rodeo queens, is it not?" Morgan was clearly enjoying herself at her expense.

"Yes, but trust me, I am no rodeo queen," said Dusty. She hadn't felt playful in a long time. She was always so serious, always to the point and on task. But she was enjoying her hike with Morgan, who was funny and relaxing to be around.

"So who is watching your horses while you are here, while you are away?"

"My neighbors. Rich and his wife Mary, they own the farm next to mine, we help each other out from time to time. Actually, I pay their niece to help on a regular basis. She's like my farmhand."

"You live on a farm?"

"I do, I love it. It's not a working farm, but I have a handful of acres that I rent out to cattle ranchers. I mostly wanted it for the land, you know, for the horses. I have a little greenhouse and space for my horses and my little pack mule for long-haul trips in the mountains. Her name is Debbie."

"Wow. That's cool. In Seattle, huh?"

"Well, actually, it's a little town about thirty miles east of Seattle."

"I see," said Morgan. "So, your family, your mom and dad are still in Caldwell?"

"Um-hum," said Dusty.

Morgan stopped and waited for Dusty to catch up. She took her time doing so. Who knew when she would be able to take a breather. Must be getting close to sunrise, she thought, as she grabbed a quick drink from one of her water bottles. The first light of the morning was making her skin glow gold.

"Are we almost there?" Dusty said.

"Pretty much. Come on." Morgan turned back toward the path, then stopped abruptly. "Whoa! Hey, did you feel that?"

"Feel what?"

"I don't know. I thought I felt something—shaking or something." Morgan cocked her head to the side.

"Could it be the ground moving from the melting of the snow, like an avalanche somewhere or something like that?"

"If it was an avalanche, we'd hear it for sure. There was a bad landslide here once though. We didn't get to come camping here that year. It was a mess. It took the Forest Service the entire summer to clean things up. The road to my uncle's cabin had to be totally rebuilt."

"It's probably just the ground thawing out," Dusty repeated.

"Yeah, you're probably right." Morgan veered off the main trail onto another hidden path. "This way. We're almost there."

A good thing, Dusty thought.

"You know," said Morgan. "The scenery is quite nice too."

"What? I…" *Shit*, thought Dusty. Morgan had caught her staring at her backside.

Morgan laughed and continued through on an unmarked trail, parting low-hanging branches.

"Here it is." Morgan poked her head through a barrier of evergreen brush, smiled and beckoned her forward.

The parting in the trees revealed an outcropping of patchy snow, fresh spring grass and thick and ancient mountain stone. There was room enough to pitch a small tent and have a fire. The best part as far as Dusty was concerned was that it was completely secluded, hidden from the main walking trail. And the view was totally unobstructed. They saw a thick blanket of rugged evergreens. Countless shades of blue and green filled the canyon below. The tops of the mountains, capped in white, glistened as the sun began its slow climb.

"I didn't realize we were this high up," Dusty said.

"Well, the lodge is at about five thousand feet," Morgan said, fiddling with her GPS watch. "We've been hiking for a little over an hour and a half. No thanks to your short legs," she smiled, "we've hiked four-point-two miles. Which puts us at about..." She trailed off as she saw how entranced Dusty was with the sight before them.

"Here it comes," said Dusty. She took in the rainbow of colors, the oranges, reds and crimsons, the wisps of cloud absorbing the sun's coloring, erasing the purples and blues of twilight. It was if she were watching Bob Ross blend the colors of a painting. "You would come out here all by yourself when you were a girl?"

"Yeah, well, with my sister." Morgan ignored the sky and focused on Dusty. "At first my parents were livid. They thought that a bear had gotten us or that we had run away, but they let us be after we told them we were watching the sunrise from our favorite spot. They had instilled in us a love and appreciation for the outdoors—how could they get angry at us?"

"There are bears here?" whispered Dusty, eyes glued to the sunrise.

Morgan didn't answer, turning to the reddening sky giving light and warmth to the world around them. With it came the chattering of little birds talking about this, that and the other. The forest was waking up and they were there, saying good morning to it.

"It's going to be a beautiful day today and a nice week for the workshop."

"Oh, yeah," sighed Dusty, "the workshop." She hoped she sounded enthusiastic. She wished she could spend the entire week at this very spot. She should have brought her laptop with her. Maybe she could come out here again during her stay. Maybe tomorrow, after her keynote? She didn't have anything else going on in between obligations. That is, if she could find the path again. Lost in her thoughts, she wasn't sure how long she had been watching the sunrise. The sound of a zipper opening broke her concentration.

"You up for a little trail mix? Not really breakfast, but I need a snack."

Dusty watched Morgan spread out a blanket on the rocky plateau and walked over to join her. She looked irresistible sitting on the little blanket. She watched Morgan remove her hat and run her hands through her wavy blonde hair, no longer styled for the classroom.

"I need a snack too. I brought some dried fruit. I picked it up at that Co-Op place. I stopped there…" *After leaving your house…* "After your class," Dusty said, wondering if her lie was obvious. The Co-Op was closer to Morgan's house than to the BSU campus. Plus, Dusty had told Morgan that she was leaving straight for McCall after her presentation. She couldn't lie worth a damn.

"Oh, yeah, I know the Co-Op," Morgan said with a smile. "Come, sit down." She patted the space next to her.

Dusty complied, letting the morning sun warm her. As she removed her hat and her puffy coat, she caught Morgan glancing at her breasts. *Well, now we're even*, she thought, as she had been caught nearly every time she had stolen glances at Morgan's body.

"So," said Morgan in between handfuls of her trail mix.

Here she goes again, thought Dusty.

"I am curious: How long have you known Teggy?"

Phew, that's an easy question. Dusty had to think a moment. "I have known her for quite some time—maybe twelve years or so." She popped a handful of nuts in her mouth. Morgan looked at her as though expecting a deeper answer. "I met her at a career fair and got a job working for her agency as an intern. I worked there until I graduated."

"And you kept in touch?"

At Morgan's encouragement, she continued. "Yeah, pretty much. I became personal friends with her after I quit working at her agency to focus on writing." There was more, of course. Dusty thought back to the week she had started working for Teggy. She had been spending the nights in the intern office when Teggy had returned to the office late one night for some files or something. Teggy had pulled out of Dusty the fact that she was bordering on homelessness, had been staying at the local youth shelter. But she wasn't going to tell that to Morgan. "She helped me tremendously through school and with my writing. She encouraged me to publish and, well, here we are."

"Yes, here we are," she said. "Does she call you Dusty too?"

Dusty laughed. "Yes, she does."

"So Dusty is your nickname?"

"Yeah. The people I lived with on the reservation—the Red Elk family that I wrote about—gave it to me. They taught me to ride horses and taught me about the outdoors and the mountains. For some reason I would always get so dusty when I rode, so Dusty kind of stuck."

"Fair enough. Dusty *is* better than being called dirty," said Morgan, laughing at herself. She stopped when she saw the look on Dusty's face. "Sorry, that wasn't funny. So, you grew up in Caldwell and went to college in Washington?"

"Yep. Where did you go to school?" said Dusty, stopping Morgan's incursion into her personal life.

"I grew up in Boise, went to Boise High and went to Boise State for undergrad, the University of Washington for graduate school, where I met Tegs, and returned to Boise State for my PhD program. Actually, it wasn't a formal PhD program yet. I had a sponsoring instructor and we designed the program together."

"And you built the department. Teggy said you started it?"

"Yes, I stayed to build the department into what it is now. It was nothing before I got there, and I've poured my heart and soul into it, into my students. Many of my graduates have gone on to work on high-level projects and for high-powered people all over the world. I really am proud of them."

"You should be proud of yourself. You are a great teacher. I mean, from what I saw." Dusty darted a nervous look at Morgan. Dusty had considered teaching before, after the success of *Reservations*. She enjoyed public speaking and had enjoyed meeting the eager and driven students she often spoke to during her book tours. But she couldn't handle the fact that for teaching you had to be *on* all the time. She had decided she was too moody for teaching, but could handle guest lecturing every now and again.

"Thanks. You're not bad with the students either—actually, you are amazing with them." Morgan seemed to be growing bolder with her interactions with Dusty. They sat in silence for a bit, basking in the sun's rising warmth.

"Did you enjoy the sunrise?" asked Morgan.

"Yes, I did, it was…stunning. Thank you for inviting me."

Morgan stood, stretched and smiled at Dusty. Dusty couldn't help but smile back, thinking about having the same view when Morgan had forced her to the chair and straddled her.

"Do you think you can make it a little farther, to the grand lookout? It's not too much further and you can see even farther in all directions. We're already halfway there. Want to keep going? Or do you have to get back?"

"Yes. I mean, no—I don't have to get back. I would love to." Dusty stood and stretched. "But can we slow down a little bit?"

"Come on, I know you can keep up with me," said Morgan.

"Your legs are way longer than mine. Seriously longer."

"Fine. We will go slower," said Morgan.

* * *

They made their way back to the main trail and headed up again. Dusty soon fell behind again and grew short of breath. Climbing mountains on foot versus on horseback was new to her. She had ridden plenty and had camped dozens of times but had always had her little mule to carry her things. Not that she was carrying that much in her backpack, just water and trail snacks She finally accepted that it was not just the altitude; Morgan was simply in much better shape.

They had been going at it for at least forty-five minutes when they felt it.

"What the hell was that?" Dusty stopped dead in her tracks, her eyes growing wide.

"I'm not sure, but we need to get the hell out of here, out from under these trees. Up there, on the trail!" Morgan said as things started falling on them from above. "Follow me. Hurry! It doesn't feel right! It's getting worse, come on!" she shouted as the trembling grew more violent. Trees were shaking and the earth was literally opening up all around them.

Dusty stayed glued to her spot as Morgan ran away from her. Everything was happening in slow motion. She saw flocks of birds retreating from the trees above her and tree limbs were shaking fiercely, dropping debris onto her. She pulled leaves and twigs from her hair and stared at them as if she had never seen such things before.

"Come on!" screamed Morgan. "Dusty! Come on, for Christ sake! We have to get out of here! Make for the open ground." Morgan threw her backpack to the ground and sprinted back for Dusty. She grabbed her hands, shaking her out of her stupor. "Snap out of it, let's go." She pushed Dusty out of the way as a massive tree branch fell, almost hitting her. The weight of the thing surely would have killed her.

"Shit." Dusty shook her head, pushing herself up, her knee throbbing from landing hard on it. She could feel blood start to wet her knee and seep through her jeans. Morgan followed behind her, then grabbed her arm and moved out in front of her, practically dragging her along. "Try to keep up. We have to get out from under the canopy!" The quaking and rumbling had become deafening as dead trees, branches and rocks fell and the mountain began to disappear from underneath them. They had to get to higher ground. The farther they went, the more destruction they saw behind them.

They had reached a clearing when they heard it: an eerie silence, followed by the loudest crash Dusty had ever heard. Directly above them, a mass of earth and snow had broken free and was headed straight for them like a freight train on the loose, smashing through everything in its path, erasing the world. They were next in its path of destruction.

"Run! Don't stop, run!" Morgan screamed at Dusty.

Dusty tried her best to keep up with Morgan, but her legs were too tired, too out of shape. "Go on, I'll be right behind you," she yelled, arms flailing. "I'm right behind you."

She was knocked to her knees again.

"No!" screamed Morgan, coming back for her again. "Get up!" She pulled Dusty to her feet once more as the massive landslide came down around them.

Dusty was thrown forward hard, her breath nearly knocked out of her. She was getting dizzy and losing her bearings. The world went yellow around her and then black. She didn't know which way was up and which way was down. Reaching out, trying to find Morgan, she felt the other woman wrap her arms around her.

"Come on," Morgan said. She pulled her toward her with such force that Dusty fell on top of her. They started to roll down the mountain.

CHAPTER FIFTEEN

Morgan came to a stop on her back, tasting blood in her mouth. The mountain around her felt eerily still. A huge plume of debris lingered in the air around her. She heard smaller rocks clattering down the mountain. She looked down the slope and spotted Dusty's orange backpack. It was still on her back, had probably protected her to some degree, but she was not moving. She tried to get up, to go to her. That was when the lights went out.

She came to later in an instant, as if woken by an alarm.

"Hel…!" Her scream was cut short, mid-shout, by the pain that was now registering on every inch of her body. Half of her body was covered in mud and rock, a sloppy mess of sludge and wetness that was heavy and cold. Slowly and in agony, she managed to sit up. She stayed that way for a moment, head in her hands, struggling to comprehend what had happened. Her vision was yellow, her head hurt and she wasn't sure where she was. Dazed, she struggled to free herself from the suction of the sludge and stand up. She got up onto one of her knees and then onto her feet, only to wince and fall back down when her left leg buckled under her.

"Damn it," she whispered. She wanted water, but her pack was nowhere to be seen.

She turned her head to look down the mountain. Dusty lay about eighty or so feet down the mountain, her body twisted in an awful way. The moment she saw her, she remembered where they were and why she was lying on the ground in pain.

"Dusty," Morgan whispered, her head hurting too much to talk any louder. "Dusty, hey, are you okay? Wake up!" She scooted on her backside down the mountain. Her left leg was next to useless, and the rest of her body was sore and stiff. Finally, she reached her. She was unconscious, but breathing.

"Dusty, hey, wake up." She worked to free the petite woman from the mud, snow and rocks covering her legs. As gently as she could, she slipped her arms out of her backpack, rolled her onto her back and brushed the debris and mud from her face. She crouched down beside her, putting her hand on her chest, finding a slow but steady heartbeat. "Dusty? Wake up, hey, come on, wake up." Nothing. Unsure what to do next, Morgan reached out to smooth the hair from her scratched face.

Dusty jumped at her touch.

"Oh," she gasped, wincing in pain. "What happened? Where am I?" She moved to grab Morgan's hand. Morgan gently held her in place.

"It's okay. Relax. It was a landslide. We were right in its path. We were lucky we didn't get completely buried." Morgan looked around. Massive boulders and jagged pieces of tree were everywhere. "We could have been impaled or crushed by a rock. Jesus! Are you okay? Can you move?"

"I think so." Dusty moved her feet and her arms, tried again to sit up and failed. "I'm a little sore. And dizzy."

"I know. Take your time. Can you believe that? I thought we were goners. We could have been buried or crushed or…" She stopped, hearing the note of hysteria in her voice.

"Hey, hey, it's all right," whispered Dusty. "We made it. We're going to be all right." Dusty managed to prop herself onto her side for a moment only to give in and lay flat on her back again.

Morgan grabbed Dusty's pack and opened it to get her water bottles out. She gave Dusty one. "Here, drink."

"Thanks," Dusty said in between sips. Morgan took the other bottle for herself, drinking half the water in one gulp— and instantly throwing it up.

"Oh, that wasn't a good idea." She felt herself beginning to fade out again, fought it long enough to see Dusty pass out and then allowed the darkness to overwhelm her again.

* * *

"Morgan? Come on. We need to go." Dusty remembered coming to earlier and getting some water. She must have blacked out again. Morgan too. She wondered how long they'd been unconscious. "Give me your phone. We need to call for help."

"Hmm?" Morgan said, eyes still closed as she worked her way up to a sitting position.

"Your phone. Do you have…Where is your backpack?"

"I have no clue. Probably under a couple of tons of rock." She looked around. "Oh, man, I thought, wow, geez, you were dead…" Her eyes closed. Her words were slurred. Dusty knew what the signs of a concussion were, and Morgan seemed to be displaying a number of them. She, on the other hand, felt fine: sore, but alert. She managed to move herself to a sitting position.

"No one is dead here." Dusty held onto Morgan's arms, steadying her. "I'm fine, and so are you, but I think you have a concussion. You're acting funny."

"Well, I freggin' fell down a mountain," she said.

"I know, Morgan. We need to get help. What hurts?"

"My ankle. And my knee—I twisted it. And my head. It's like I drank a fifth of tequila. I was really dizzy when I woke up. It took me a while to remember where I was, but…" Morgan rubbed her head with her hands.

"Shit, come on, let's get up," Dusty said. "We've got to figure out what to do. The ground, it's not safe. The trail—Jesus, the mountainside—it's completely gone." Dusty helped Morgan struggle to her feet.

"If I'd known there was a danger of a landslide, that things weren't safe up here, I never would have... I can't believe I almost killed Destiny del Carmen, the writer," said Morgan, slowly, her eyes widening.

"Oh, please," said Dusty, not taking the comment seriously until she looked over and saw Morgan's eyes pool with tears. "No, hey, it's okay. This"—she said, looking all around—"is not your fault. I also think it was more than a landslide. It felt like an earthquake. Remember the shaking we felt earlier this morning? This could have been another one or an aftershock." Morgan nodded, but her hands were shaking and her eyes were still dropping a couple of tears. Dusty looked up at her. "How were you to know? You can't predict something like this; I didn't see any signs or notices about landslide warnings. Did you?"

"No," she said, looking Dusty up and down. "Can you get up?"

"Yeah, I think so," said Dusty, wincing as she tried to prop herself up with her right hand. "Shit, that hurts."

"Oh, are you okay?"

"Yes, but that's my good hand."

Morgan smiled as she wiped her tears away. "It sure is your good hand."

"My 'good hand'?" Dusty felt a flush rise within her.

"Oh shit, did I say that out loud?" Morgan laughed at herself.

"Yes, you did. It's my writing hand, my...my main typing hand, and I, I paint a little," Dusty said, hearing Morgan's laugh building. "Jesus, you're worse than I am."

"I'm sorry, but I feel funny."

"I know. You probably have a concussion. We need to keep going and find help. Get back down to the lodge or something."

"Agreed." Morgan zipped the water bottles back into the backpack. "Come on. Let's get up. Let's make for higher ground. We can't go back down there." She motioned to the mess below.

The women helped each other to their feet. Morgan's body braced Dusty's as she slowly got up, dizzy and unsteady. Damn, Morgan felt good. Even after almost getting run over by a landslide, contact with her caused Dusty's heart to race.

She looked at herself and then at Morgan. Both of them were total messes. The muddy slurry that the slide had left behind was in their hair and on their clothes—inside their clothes. Scratches covered Morgan's face and, judging from the stinging she felt there, probably her own as well. Bruises were becoming evident. Their coats were ripped and pant legs torn, and mud filled their boots. But they were alive. And they could walk—if they held onto each other.

They decided they would try for Morgan's uncle's cabin rather than go back down. That would be too dangerous; landslides were notorious for sliding again at the faintest disturbance.

"We should be able to make it to my uncle's cabin in a few hours, though without the trail as a guide it's going to be difficult." Morgan looked at her GPS watch, which was still working they'd been glad to discover. "It's going to be about another mile or so…that way." She pointed. "He has a radio that we can use to call for help."

"Oh, thank God. Can you walk? Can you do it?" Dusty asked. Morgan's face was pale and awash in pain, and she was limping pretty badly at each step.

"Yes, as long as we go slow."

"Slow I can do," said Dusty.

CHAPTER SIXTEEN

They felt rumbling beneath their feet every so often as they made their way at a snail's pace toward the cabin. After a pause each time to stare at each other with wide eyes at the thought of having to try to again get quickly out of harm's way, they kept moving, working their way around and through the rock, earth and muddy snow, branches and boulders, tree roots and shrubs that lay littered around them. The birds they'd heard chattering at sunrise were silent. All they heard now was the creaking of the ground and the rocks crunching under their feet.

It was going to be a long trek; the trail was mostly mud. Hearing Morgan's slight whimpering as they negotiated some of the rougher terrain, Dusty held on to her tighter to support her.

"How are you holding up?" asked Dusty.

"I'll make it," Morgan said, but Dusty had to practically carry her over some of the rougher patches, and they had to stop often for her to rest. According to Morgan's watch, it had been nearly six hours since they left their cabins. They had spent an hour and a half getting to the lookout, two hours watching the sun come up and eating breakfast, and another forty-five minutes hiking toward the summit when the landslide nearly swallowed them whole. They didn't think they had been passed out for more than twenty minutes, all told, but at their current rate the trek to the cabin would get them there closer to late afternoon, later than that if they had to backtrack many more times to go around piles of debris and logs.

* * *

It was starting to get cold and their bodies were crying out in pain at what they were putting them through. Morgan hoped to God that her uncle's cabin had been spared and that it had edible food and water as well as a first-aid kit. Dusty's pants and forehead were bloody. She wondered if she looked as battered as Dusty did. She wasn't looking forward to removing her boot to examine her ankle.

"There." Morgan pointed. "That way, up over that ridge. We're almost there." A small A-frame cabin with an aluminum roof was nestled neatly among the trees. The land around it looked different than the wooded area they had come from. But that was characteristic of the Payette National Forest. There were so many zones to explore. Dry desert grasslands bordered thick forested areas and what looked like rangeland. There were fewer trees, different types of trees and plants and in the distance behind the cabin a massive lake still partially filled with snow in the middle. She could see other cabins in the far distance. The smell of crisp cold air filled her lungs. It was cleansing to her and reminded her of home.

"Jesus, look at that," said Morgan, pointing to a large downed tree limb behind the cabin. "That was lucky."

"No kidding," said Dusty.

"It looks like it nailed the firewood shed. The cabin looks fine though, doesn't it?"

"Yeah, it does. Come on, almost there," said Dusty, now fully supporting Morgan as they hobbled toward the cabin. Dusty let go of her for a moment as she opened the door to a screened-off mudroom preceding the door to the cabin. She helped Morgan settle on the wooden bench and tried the door. Nothing. She sat back down to catch her breath.

Morgan laughed. "No, it wouldn't be open. I told you we would have to break in."

"Do we really need to break in or would there be a hidden key somewhere?" Dusty looked under the entry mat and, standing on the tip of her toes, felt above the doorframe.

"Oh yes." Morgan's voice was groggy. "There is a metal fish. It's a trout, a rainbow trout. Technically a steelhead…"

"Yes, okay, it's a fish and…"

"Well, aren't we Little Miss Impatient?"

"Sorry. Go on."

"On the shed, nailed over the doorframe of that little shack around back." Morgan closed her eyes as she let her body rest against the side of the cabin. "There may be a key nestled behind the fish. Hopefully he still keeps it there and the tree didn't bury it when it took the shed down. If it's not there, you're going to have to crawl through the window to let us in."

"I'll see what I can find."

* * *

Dusty headed around back. She was stunned by the damage she found there. Thank God that hadn't happened to the cabin. She didn't know if they had the strength to do what it would take to rough it up here until help came. Assuming anyone knew they needed help and came to look for them.

"Are you okay? Have you found anything?"

"Oh yes, the fish. That's what I'm looking for," Dusty muttered to herself. "Yeah, it's a mess back here. One sec," she yelled. She looked up and spotted the fish. "Really?" she groaned. It was nailed to the entryway, which was about the only part of the shed left standing. But it was too high for her to reach.

"Tell me you found it," Morgan said eagerly.

"I found it, but I can't reach it. I'm going to need that bench you're sitting on. It's the only part of the damn shack that the tree branch didn't manage to knock down. At least the firewood is going to be easy to get to." Dusty returned and noted the amused look on Morgan's face. "What?"

"Yes, of course. I forgot. Your legs are shorter than mine."

Dusty gave her a sour look. "The bench," she demanded, grabbing Morgan's hands, gently pulling her to her feet, loving the way Morgan held on to her as she did so. Dusty grabbed the bench and started wrestling it through the narrow entry.

Morgan winced when she put her weight on her ankle but was still laughing as she leaned against the cabin door.

"I don't feel sorry for you," said Dusty, barely avoiding tumbling over the long awkward bench. That drew an even louder laugh from the other woman.

"I'm sorry, I'm sorry," she heard from afar.

"Jesus, Joseph and Mary," Dusty muttered. But finally she got the bench in place, stood on it and felt around until the key was in her hand. She presented it triumphantly to Morgan. The other woman's smile made Dusty feel like everything was going to be okay.

CHAPTER SEVENTEEN

"We need to find the radio," said Morgan as she retreated to the back of the cabin. "But, first things first. I've got to use the ladies' room."

"Do you need help?" said Dusty, then was embarrassed at what she asked.

"No, I'm fine. Make yourself at home."

Drawing open the curtains of one of the windows, Dusty let the remaining daylight into the small cabin and had a good look around. A large futon-type couch faced a stone fireplace. Above its mantel hung an antique-looking rifle. "Hope we won't need that," she muttered to herself, chuckling at the thought of having to hunt and fish for their food. By the looks of it, the couch turned into a bed. She spotted and then climbed a wooden ladder as best she could given her sprained wrist, muttering a string of curses as she made her ascent. She poked her head up far enough to see that it led to a small loft, complete with a twin bed. She smiled, relieved that there were two sleeping spaces, one upstairs and one down. "Cozy," she whispered as she climbed back down. She hoped help would come for them before it got too cozy.

Behind the couch was a small dining table, four handmade wooden chairs and a tiny galley kitchen. Pots hung from a rack on the wall. A large wood stove with two small burners atop and a sink with a pump-style faucet took up a good part of the rest of the cabin.

Next to the wood stove sat an old cast-iron tub. "This is straight-up *Little House on the Prairie*-style, isn't it," she yelled, wondering how in the world they got the heavy thing up the mountain. She was glad they made the effort. A hot bath would feel nice. She ran her hands through her hair, the mud and twigs she found there reminding her that she'd nearly gotten completely buried by a landslide.

Opposite the fireplace was a narrow bookcase that held books, playing cards, metal tins, odds and ends, games and an assortment of photos, one of which was of two little girls. Dusty assumed they were Morgan and her sister.

Her eyes were drawn to a long rug in the hallway. She moved it out of the way, revealing a hidden door in the floor. She cranked open the hatch. Not daring to go any further, she got down on her knees, looking into pitch black below.

"Morgan!" she yelled, startled as the other woman suddenly appeared. "Oh, hey, there is a cellar or something down here."

"Yeah, that's the bunker. The radio and supplies should be down there. Hopefully there are painkillers and food. Who knows how long we will need to wait for help."

"What do you mean? If it's a landslide, couldn't they bring a four-wheeler or a chopper or something up here for us?"

"I don't know," Morgan said. "When the landslide happened years and years ago—the one I was telling you about—it took them all spring and summer to fix the service road and hiking trails. Then again, we are stuck here, and we're injured. They've got to make a special rescue for us."

"Jesus, I hope so," said Dusty, thinking she was probably coming across as pretty petulant. "I don't want to have to hunt and fish for food for us." She laughed, hoping Morgan couldn't get a read on her real concerns.

"Well, since we're stuck here, and given the circumstances, maybe they can bring a rescue helicopter in. I don't know." Morgan paused. Dusty wondered what she was thinking. "Well, let's see what we have to work with. Go on, get down there."

"Down there? I'm not going down there without a flashlight or a candle or something."

"Oh, yeah, that would help, wouldn't it?" said Morgan, smiling.

"Most definitely. It's pitch black down there. I could twist my ankle or something. One of us needs to be able to walk." She shivered at the cold that emanated from the space below. "Do you think there is a heater down there too? It's freezing cold. Aren't cabins supposed to be cozy?"

"They can be, but we've got to light some fires, you know."

"No. Not really."

Morgan motioned to the kitchen. "Let's get some light on the subject. There, on the bookshelf, that wind-up looking thing is a decent flashlight."

Dusty got up to retrieve it, gave it a few cranks and shone it into the space below.

"The first thing you want to do is locate the breaker to the cabin. It should be right there, to the right, you can't miss it, it's just like what you would have at home, only there is one breaker for the entire cabin. Hopefully things are still in good shape."

"Here goes. Wish me luck." She took each step warily. When she reached the bottom, she drew in her breath in awe. She couldn't see a lot but what she could see was choice. "Wow, no offense," she said, starting to explore the room, "but the man *is* paranoid, isn't he?" She laughed. "Is this the breaker?" She gave it a flip. "Nothing happened."

"Turn the light on, the little switch, looks like a button." The lightbulb flickered to life, slowly getting brighter as it warmed up.

"Wow. Magic?"

"Solar panels on the roof." She made an upward motion with her hand.

"So rad!" She shone her flashlight over the walls. "Hey-hey, there's whiskey on them thar' shelves."

"Great, we will be just fine now," said Morgan. "What else? Do you see any semblance of a first-aid kit or water—you know, those minor essentials? Any food? Oh, and the radio...did you see it?"

Minor essentials! The man had enough canned goods to feed a small army for over a year. There were packages of dehydrated food, army-issued MREs. Blankets and other dry goods were sealed in vacuum packaging, though the few jugs of water that she found were frozen solid and there were not very many of them. However there was whiskey, enough whiskey and other spirits to get said army through the apocalypse. Candles, large oil lamps, more wind-up flashlights, a hefty-looking first-aid kit and, of course, a shotgun, ammo, tools and other such necessities. And the radio.

"There's water," she yelled to Morgan. "But it's frozen. And there isn't that much of it."

"It's okay, we have a pump. We just need to boil the first batch or two."

"I found the first-aid kit," she said, looking up at Morgan as she made her way back up toward daylight. "And this." She pulled out the bottle that had been tucked under her left arm. "I think we will be all right here for a day or two. Or a year."

"Oh yes, the essentials," said Morgan, as she eyed the whiskey.

"Tequila—that sounds better to me right now, but I'll settle for this. God, I am so sore." Dusty stretched her arms and rolled her head. She opened the first-aid kit and found painkilling pills in a package. "Take these." She handed over the pills and the whiskey.

She went back down and returned with a box holding cans of corn and beans and a few plastic bags with freeze-dried tomatoes, soups and herbs. "For dinner," she said. The box also held towels sealed in a plastic pouch and a couple of blankets. She went down again and came back with the large box that held the radio.

Dusty carefully closed the hatch. "Let's check out that radio," she said. "Do you know how to use it?" She watched Morgan remove the radio from the box and connect the components. It was powered by the flashlight's hand crank.

"This thing takes forever to charge," Morgan said. "When it is charged, its power doesn't last long, so let's hope we make contact soon with someone that can help us."

"Don't you need, like, a big-ass antenna for that to work?"

"There is a big-ass antenna built into one of the trees out back. Or there was. I am hoping it didn't sustain any damage from that downed limb. The thing about my Uncle Mike is that the man knows how to rough it."

She wound and wound the charger until it gave the radio the charge it needed. Dusty was mesmerized by Morgan's familiarity with the complicated-looking equipment.

"I'll try the emergency line and see what I can get. Here goes. Wish us luck." Morgan pressed down the speaker switch. "This is Morgan West. We were caught in the landslide earlier this morning. We need assistance. Do you copy? Over."

The women looked at each other intently, hearing only static. Morgan continued to wind the charger in between transmissions.

"Hello, this is Morgan West. Me...and another person were staying at the Bear Creek Cabins. We were out hiking early this morning and were caught in a landslide. We need assistance. Do you copy? Over."

Dusty walked slowly toward Morgan, joining her at the small table, noting how beautiful she looked despite her dirty face and disheveled clothes and hair. Dusty enjoyed the look of concentration on Morgan's face as she fiddled with the knobs, holding the radio's microphone tightly in her hand. Again, only fuzzy static came through the radio frequency. And then...

"This is McCall District Ranger Station. You are coming in loud and clear. Can you repeat your situation? Over."

Dusty's trance was broken at the other voice coming through the radio. Her eyes met Morgan's. They held each other for a beat until Morgan responded.

"Copy, McCall. This is Morgan West and"—she paused— "Destiny del Carmen. We were part of the workshop that is being held at the Bear Creek Cabins. We were on a hike early this morning up toward Cub Ridge when we got caught in the landslide. Over."

"Copy that. Are either of you seriously injured? Over."

Dusty saw Morgan hesitate. Why wasn't she answering the ranger? Surely she realized how dangerous head injuries could be. If she truly had a concussion, even a mild one, she should play it up and get them the hell off the mountain. She'd get the medical care she needed and—

And it would get them out of this damned situation before one of them gave in and yielded to the other. Dusty's eyes homed in on the scratch on Morgan's brow then dropped down to her mouth. She could nearly feel those lips on hers, on her body. Would they feel the same a second time?

Was Morgan weighing the same considerations? She was biting her lower lip gingerly and then running her tongue across it. Was she as conflicted? Static from the radio jarred them into action.

"I repeat, is there anyone with you that is seriously injured? Over."

When Morgan keyed the radio and responded, she played down her injuries, ignoring the worried looks that Dusty was shooting at her.

"McCall, no, no one here is seriously injured. A few bumps and scratches, twisted ankles. I might have a mild concussion, nothing major. I have first-aid supplies with me. What happened this morning with the landslide? No one said anything about the land here being unstable. There were no warnings when we checked into the park. Over."

"There was a magnitude three-point-two earthquake at six fifteen this morning. A mild one, but it triggered a number of landslides on the mountain, as did some of the aftershocks. You two were lucky you were out hiking so early. You must have been up over six thousand feet when it hit?" Morgan nodded at Dusty. "There is a bad mess on the mountain. We're not sure yet how far the destruction has reached… There were casualties at the lodge. Over."

The two women looked at each other with concern, faces ashen at what they'd heard. "Casualties," they whispered, genuine concern in their eyes. Dusty remembered the woman whose book she had signed when she had checked in. She hoped she was alive and well.

"McCall, should we try to make it down the mountain? Over."

"No, do not. Repeat, do not. There have been tremors all morning. The ground is not safe and the mud is three feet thick in places. You're going to need a rescue team to get out of there. How are you transmitting, Morgan? You said you were up by Cub Ridge—did you by chance reach the cabins south of Salmon Run Lookout? You are Morgan West, did you say? Over."

"Yes, Morgan West. We are in Mike West's cabin. He's my uncle. We were in the area watching the sunrise, making our way to the Salmon Run Lookout. Over."

"Morgan, do you have water and food there to last for a little bit? Over." The women's eyes met again. "Yes, actually we have a good supply of stuff here," said Morgan, her eyes glued to Dusty's. "Why? How long will it be before we can get off the mountain? Over."

"All of our resources are being tied up with the injured and mess down here. We're getting aid from neighboring counties. You two are going to have to be prepared for staying up there for at least two or three, maybe four days, before we can get aid to you. And since you aren't in a true emergency situation—no one is severely hurt and you have shelter, food and water—you are low on the list to be rescued. You're going to have to sit tight. Can you do that? Over."

"You're fucking kidding me," said Dusty, giving Morgan a pleading look as she ran her hurt hand through her hair, wincing at the pain that caused. She stood up and walked over to the window, shaking her head in disbelief. She was not sure she would be able to live with Morgan for the next twenty-four hours and not rip her clothes off. And what good would that do? She did not want anything more than their one-night stand. She did not want to let her emotions take her to a place she couldn't return from. She didn't have it in her.

Dusty didn't know how Morgan felt about their situation, but she had clearly picked up on Dusty's objection to being stranded. "You're kidding me, McCall! Three or four days? Over."

"No, I'm not kidding. You two are lucky that you were able to make it to the cabin. There were other people on that trail that weren't so lucky, including school kids on a snow-tubing field trip this morning. We haven't even begun to determine the full extent of the injuries there. We can't spare any air support right now, so we will have to come in on four-wheelers to get you. That will take some time. I hope you can understand. Are there any people you want us to contact to let them know you two are alive and well? Over."

"Stand by, McCall. Over."

"McCall standing by. Over."

Morgan looked at Dusty and wound the charger. "Sorry, Dusty. There is Teggy. I don't have her phone number, but they can probably look it up. Is there anyone else you want to notify, anyone else who needs to know you are okay?"

"Just Teggy," Dusty said as she walked back outside, not wanting to listen to the rest of the radio transmission. She needed space. "Unfuckingbelievable." She paced in the enclosed porch. She shouldn't have let Teggy guilt her into this trip. Now look where she was. She was hurt, tired and stuck here with a woman who was getting into her head, a woman who was also hurt and no doubt would need her help. She didn't know how to care for someone else; she could barely take care of herself of late. All she had wanted to do was go on a hike with the woman, not spend three days with her.

No, she didn't want anything more to do with Professor West—she was afraid of what she was feeling, afraid of the look in Morgan's eyes and, more so, what she saw in them. She started thinking through the possibilities of trying to make it down the mountain on her own.

She walked out toward the little shack in the back of the cabin, surveying the land around her, seeing nothing but beauty.

Most everything around the cabin, save for the little shack, had been unaffected by the earthquake and landslide. She folded her arms around herself. The day was growing cold as the sun started making its descent. She took a deep breath. Jesus, she was acting like a child. She should probably get back into the cabin to help get a fire going and make something for them to eat. She should get back inside and face the situation instead of running from it.

That would be a first for her.

CHAPTER EIGHTEEN

Morgan was seated at the little table, leg stretched out, eyes closed, head hung low, her hand still gripping the radio. She was shivering. The sound of the mudroom door opening signaled that Dusty had not run off entirely. She looked up to see her return, looking somewhat calmer than when she had left.

"Morgan? Hey, are you all right? Does your head still hurt?"

"Yes, I mean, no, my head, I feel better." She nodded.

"What did the ranger say?"

Morgan ignored Dusty's question. "What are the odds that we were hiking up here the moment the earthquake hit? I'm having a hard time wrapping my mind around everything. It's unreal." She sighed, noticing how scared Dusty looked. Dusty's eyes were drawn down, defeated.

"Hey, Dusty, it's going to be okay. We're going to get rescued. It's three or four days. We have food and water. Oh, and excellent whiskey, and my uncle probably has a joint or two down there. How bad can it be?" Morgan so wanted to make Dusty feel better. She had succeeded in her last attempt to do so. But this time was different. Dusty needed something else. What, she didn't know.

"No, I know," Dusty said, shaking her head. "I know, I wish...I...don't want to be here."

"Of course you don't. Neither do I. I have a family down there and a life. We're in the same boat here, Destiny. It's okay." She was confused and a little hurt at Dusty's reaction. "You don't have to explain, I understand." She lied.

* * *

Dusty sighed and wished she could go to Morgan and hold her, say she was sorry for how she was acting, explain why. But she couldn't. She didn't know how. There were a lot of things she didn't know how to do when it came to her emotions. A heart-to-heart with another woman usually ended in her getting yelled at, and she didn't want to cause a scene tonight. "No, it's not like that. I don't know how—"

"How to what? Make a fire? How to...deal with shit?" Morgan said. "You know what, forget it. I'll get the fire going. I'll get everything ready. Don't worry about anything but yourself." Morgan tried to get up, moaned in pain and sat right back down. She breathed deeply, eyes closed. Her hands massaged her forehead. "Fuck," she said, extending her leg, reaching for it. She was clearly in pain.

"I didn't mean it like that," said Dusty, now feeling horrible. "Morgan, I...I don't know how...to take care of someone else, how to take care of you, with your hurt ankle. You're in pain. You have a concussion. I don't know what to do to make you feel better."

She turned to avoid Morgan's eyes. She had told her the truth—she was afraid she would totally screw up caring for Morgan—but not the whole truth. The fact was she was scared to death of being with Morgan for three or four days, scared to death of how desperately she wanted to take her into her arms and hold and kiss her. The best thing to do probably was to leave, get the hell out of town and get on with her life—away from Morgan. That had been the plan all along—and now this.

"Fuck." Morgan held her head in her hands. "Dusty, oh, Jesus, I'm sorry." She looked up. "It's going to be fine. We will help each other out. We will take care of each other, okay? I'll look out for you and you look out for me. God, I am so sorry! I feel like shit and I'm hurt and tired. I don't do hurt and tired very well, and I took it out on you. Please—you don't have to be scared, all right?"

Dusty nodded her head to indicate that she understood and ran her hand through her hair, scattering dried mud everywhere. "It's fine. I totally deserved that. I don't know why I reacted that way." She was lying. Deep down she knew the reason why.

"No, I had absolutely no right to talk to you like that. I'm sorry."

"I'll think of it as a side effect of your concussion." Dusty smiled.

"Thank you."

"Well, what should we do now?"

"Get the firewood from out back. Bring as much of it as you can to the closed-off porch before it gets dark. Let's get a fire started before we freeze to death. And did you see any clothes we could use and more blankets and stuff in the bunker?"

"Yes, I'll get them after I get the wood," said Dusty.

"Before you go out, we need to get the pump going. Hope it's not frozen solid."

Morgan went to work on the pump, priming it with the water remaining in the bottle in Dusty's backpack. "If this doesn't work, we may have to resort to using the whiskey," she joked, starting to pump the handle. "If that happens, for God's sake never let Uncle Mike know." The pump gurgled and groaned as she tried to wake it from its slumber.

"Thank goodness," they said in unison as the pump began to splash and spit water into the basin. "Can you manage the rest?" asked Morgan, exhausted by her efforts.

"Manage to boil water? I think so," Dusty said with a smile, getting a laugh from Morgan in return.

"Thank you. I wish I could help more at the moment. I am next to useless and it's driving me nuts."

"It's all right. You're hurt. I really can manage everything."

* * *

Nearly an hour later, Dusty had finished their chores. Morgan watched her brush off her hands and bend to catch her breath. "There should be enough firewood there for tonight."

Before starting the fires, she got two more painkillers from the first-aid kit. "Here, you should take a couple more. They should help—they usually do when I have a hangover." She chuckled and took two for herself.

"Thanks," said Morgan, chasing the pills with whiskey since the water they had pumped was sitting in a kettle on the wood stove, waiting to be boiled. She downed it all in one shot, throwing her head back dramatically and slamming the bottle on the table.

Deciding to put off taking her pills until she could wash them down with water, Dusty located the fireplace flue and opened it, put logs and kindling into the firebox, and put a match to them. Soon warmth filled the small place. Wanting to lighten the mood, she got up and took down the photo of the two little girls. "Is one of these you?"

"Yes," Morgan said with a chuckle. "Me and my sister Maria when we were seven and nine, I think. I am the little one. Do you have brothers and sisters?"

At Dusty's shake of her head, Morgan decided to let it be. Dusty was obviously closed off about her family for some reason or another and she didn't want to get into it. She would tell her what she wanted when she was ready. Besides, she had made it very clear that she didn't want anything from her anyway. Why push it? Why go there?

Morgan adjusted herself in the hard chair, wincing at the pain. "Time will fly by, Dusty. You'll see. It won't be that bad." She was lying, of course. Despite the hot and cold aura Dusty had given off all day, there was something about the writer that she wanted more of, something that went deeper than the physical need she had been wrestling with since Dusty had entered her classroom and captivated her all over again. Dusty had been giving her lingering looks all day. Looks that had only served to oxygenate the embers that had been lit within her the night they had met. Would she be able to get through the next few days without throwing herself at Dusty as she had done the night they had met?

"I know, and I'm sorry for acting, yet again, like a complete ass. You were right back at the lodge." Dusty loaded logs into the wood stove. "It took me less than a day to do something to piss you off again. I owe you a drink." She smiled.

"Oh, I shouldn't have said that. Anyway, I got you back with my outburst earlier."

"So we're even, then?"

"Yeah," Morgan said, smiling as she watched Dusty light the match and throw it into the wood stove. She felt the fire come alive.

CHAPTER NINETEEN

The sun was long gone and fires in the fireplace and the stove were ablaze, providing much needed comforting warmth. A couple of oil-powered lanterns provided the majority of the lighting. The cabin felt completely peaceful despite the events of the day. Dusty walked over to Morgan and smiled down at her. Taking a deep breath, she offered her hands to help Morgan from her chair.

"Come here to the couch. Let's get your clothes off."

"My clothes off?" Morgan said, shock on her face.

"Oh God, that's not what I meant. I mean your shoes and socks, to look at your ankle," Dusty fumbled, taking a deep breath to compose herself. "We need to take a look at your ankle to see what we've got. Who knows, maybe I will need to do surgery."

"Surgery? Oh God."

"Yeah, but don't worry, I am very capable. I have had to sew up a horse or two in my time on the trail."

"So you think I'm a horse?" said Morgan as she reached for Dusty's hands and let herself be pulled up. The charge she felt as Morgan held on to her nearly made Dusty forget the events of the day. Dusty led her to the couch and let her down gently, placing her arm tightly around her back as she sat. She felt Morgan's breathing hitch. "Are you okay?"

"Fine."

Dusty sat in silence as she gently removed Morgan's boots.

"Let's see your ankle. Let's get that sock off."

"I can take off my own sock." Morgan tried to pull her leg up to reach her foot but fell back in obvious pain. Shifting her hips, she slid down and extended her leg out to rest on Dusty's knees as the other woman sat on the ledge of the fireplace. *Jesus*, thought Dusty, an image of Morgan offering herself to her the other night flashing through her mind.

When Dusty picked up her ankle, Morgan lifted her hips at the pain and moaned, her hands clutching the futon she was sitting on.

"It's pretty swollen. Ready for the sock?"

"Yes, just…go slow," she said, a grimace on her face.

Dusty reached over to retrieve the whiskey. "Here, take a swig."

Morgan did as she was told and took a long gulp from the bottle before nestling it between her legs. "Oh, that's good," she said. "It tastes like straight-up cinnamon."

"Sounds delightful. Ready?"

"Ready as I'll ever be."

Dusty gently peeled her sock off and they surveyed the damage. The ankle was purple, fat and puffy.

"Jesus, ouch. It's pretty swollen. Can you move it, like from side to side, up and down?" asked Dusty, holding Morgan's foot gently in her hands, making note of toenails painted gold. She didn't remember seeing those on Saturday, but then again, she had been…distracted by other things. Things she shouldn't be thinking of now, she reminded herself.

"Yes, I can. I don't think it is broken. I mean, I was able to walk here on it. I think it's only a really bad sprain. I have twisted this ankle before." She looked to meet Dusty's eyes and smiled. "I think I will live."

"I think you will too."

"How is your...typing hand?" Morgan said, trying not to laugh.

"It actually doesn't hurt too much. I didn't knock it too hard, I guess. I'm fine, though a hot bath would probably do us both good. I can draw one for you first and after I can make us something to eat."

"Oh, a hot bath would help anything right about now." Morgan shifted herself back up against the couch, taking another hearty swig from the bottle of whiskey, settling it back between her legs only to see Dusty reach down to grab it on her way to get the water ready. She placed her hands atop Dusty's.

"Stop."

"What?" said Dusty, her eyes looking deep into Morgan's.

"Do you know what you are about to drink?"

"Uh, whiskey?"

"That isn't just any whiskey. This is Johnny Walker Blue Label."

Dusty slowly pulled the bottle from between Morgan's legs, poured some into a cup, sniffed it and took a taste.

"Oh wow, yeah, that is good." Dusty let out a deep breath from her lungs. "It tastes like...cedar. I love it." She poured herself another taste. "Oh, it's like fire."

"Told you." Morgan smiled at Dusty.

"I bet your uncle paid a fortune to get plumbing into this cabin," said Dusty as she rinsed out the tub and readied Morgan's bath. She had found the soap, towels and—thankfully—toothbrushes in the bunker below.

"He put a lot of his money into it. He does a lot of fishing here. And he never married, so this was like his baby. He spends more time here than in his own home. My family used it quite a lot when I was little too, but my parents preferred to camp in tents. You know, roughing it. But we spent a lot of time in here too."

While Morgan sipped the whiskey, Dusty worked on heating the water for their baths, diluting cold water from the pump with kettles of boiling water. Eventually the tub became a steaming pool of relaxation. They very well could have been in a resort in the French Riviera.

"Okay." Dusty cleared her throat. She rubbed her hands up and down her thighs. "It's ready for you. I'll, um…I can wait in the loft so you can have your privacy. I mean, I'm sure…"

"You see that line over there?" said Morgan, motioning to a length of rope that was hanging in a neat circle on the wall. "It gets strung up from there to there." She motioned with her finger. "After it's hung, clip on a sheet, and voilà, privacy! Besides, it's not like you haven't seen me naked before."

Dusty hoped the look on her face didn't reveal how hot that single comment had caused her to feel inside. Apparently she had failed, judging by the teasing look on Morgan's face.

This is going to be a long three to four days at this rate, she thought. *Very, very long.*

While Morgan was bathing, Dusty got more wood from the porch and stocked both the fireplace in the living room and the wood stove. She was careful to avoid stealing glances at Morgan soaking in the tub—even though all the moaning she was doing at the obvious pleasure she was getting from the hot soak made that damn near impossible. She also retreated to the bunker several times for more blankets, clothing and other odds and ends that would make their first night more comfortable. She made up the loft bed and piled blankets and pillows on the futon.

As she was going about her tasks, though, she couldn't help but catch glimpses of Morgan's body through the curtain she had hung. The flicker of the light from the fireplace was casting her tantalizing shadow here and there on the walls throughout the small cabin. Dusty didn't know how long she would be able to avoid acting on her feelings with this kind of temptation being dangled in front of her all the time. She wondered if Morgan knew what she was doing to her.

After Morgan got dressed, Dusty got her settled on the couch, helping her rest her leg on one of the little kitchen chairs, stacking a couple of pillows on top so Morgan could elevate her leg and putting small towels of ice-cold water on her foot to bring the swelling down. The slipping and sliding they'd done on the way to the cabin had probably made the original injury ten times worse.

After Dusty had bathed and tended to her own scrapes and cuts, she dressed in the same outfit as Morgan, oversized flannel button-ups that belonged to her uncle, oversized boxer shorts, and large, but comfy sweatpants.

Before joining Morgan on the couch, Dusty washed their dirty clothes and hung them to dry on a rope strung over the wood stove. She joined Morgan by the fire, which was blazing, and topped off their glasses. Somewhere along the line the idea of making and eating dinner had been shelved in favor of more trail mix and whiskey.

* * *

"I feel a lot better, thanks to your prescription of painkillers and alcohol," said Morgan, breaking the comfortable silence they'd been enjoying. Dusty gave her a wan smile in return.

"Thank *you*," she whispered, her eyes fixed on her little glass of whiskey.

"For what? I should be thanking you. I would probably still be sitting on the porch, freezing cold by now, if it weren't for you," Morgan said.

"You saved my life today," Dusty said. "I freaked out back there. I felt the mountain shaking and I froze. I froze. I was so scared." She found the courage to look at Morgan. She was even more beautiful dressed in those baggy clothes. The flannel shirt, which wasn't fully buttoned, had shifted, leaving her right shoulder bare. Dusty could see her chest rising up and down as she breathed. Her skin was glowing warm in the fire's flame. "Thank you."

"Don't worry about it. You would have done the same thing if that was me back there." Morgan traced the rim of her glass with her fingers, taking another swig of the whiskey and giving a little gasp as the liquid fire went down her throat.

"I mean it," said Dusty, touching Morgan's thigh and stilling all movement. Their eyes met, and a growing storm stirred in Dusty's chest. She quickly pulled her hand away. Taking a deep breath, she continued, "Jesus, an earthquake. I hope the people at the lodge are okay. The ranger said there were casualties."

"Yeah, I can't stop thinking about what happened. My parents, they worry so much. My dad, he gets so stressed out. I know for a fact that they are worried about me. I hope the rangers passed on word about where I am, but there is nothing I can do to assure them that I'm okay. That sounds selfish of me, doesn't it?"

"No, I don't think so. I mean, maybe. If you were at the lodge you would be there taking care of things, but instead you're stuck here, with me, not knowing what is going on."

Tears welled up in Morgan's eyes. "I'm sorry, I'm not usually a crier," she said as she wiped her tears with the end of her shirt sleeves. "Actually, that's not true. I am a crier, I cry at just about everything, a sad movie—a happy movie—I'll cry." She laughed.

"No, hey. It's okay. No need to apologize. It must be difficult for you to be stuck up here not able to communicate with your family and friends. Not knowing how widespread the damage is. I mean, your whole life is down there. I wish I could do something to make it a little better."

"Thank you, Dusty," Morgan said, tears still wet on her face. Dusty sat back sipping her whiskey, letting the moments tick by. Before long she noticed that Morgan's eyes had closed.

Dusty took the empty glass from Morgan's hand and stared at her, not knowing what to do next. Should she wake her up so she could help her shift the futon to the bed setting? No. Best to let her just sleep.

She moved Morgan's body fully onto the futon, getting a pillow for her head and one for her foot, covered her with several blankets and threw a couple of logs into the fireplace so she wouldn't freeze in the middle of the night. She looked upon her sleeping form, taking advantage of the opportunity to finally get a good look at her.

Her golden hair lay against her face, still damp from her soak in the tub. Her eye lashes were dark, a beautiful contrast to her hair. And that sexy beauty mark on her upper lip—Dusty just wanted to kiss it.

Morgan's chest rose as she took soft breaths. She looked so at peace, so unlike the woman who had so completely dominated her not that long ago. Dusty remembered how their bodies fit together—how they had used each other for all they were worth. She wished she could join Morgan on the futon and hold her all night long and wake up next to her. Instead she made her way to the loft. It would be wise to get some rest herself. It had been a long and crazy day, but she was still wired.

CHAPTER TWENTY

When Morgan awoke early the next morning, she was unaware at first of where she was. Then it all flooded back, along with a pounding headache. As she got up, she was reminded that the day before she and Dusty had consumed only trail mix and snacks—and a lot of whiskey.

She rose and tested her ankle. It hurt badly, but less than the day before. She would need to continue to take it easy. Her whole body was aching from all that had happened. She called for Dusty. Nothing. She looked out the little window in the cabin door and found her sitting in the enclosed area with a coffee mug in her hand.

Morgan retreated to the kitchen and discovered that Dusty had brought up breakfast items from the bunker. She found powdered eggs, a bag of smoked tomatoes, oil, MRE potatoes and a pouch of herbs sitting on the little table. She went to work. Dusty opened the door a few minutes later.

"Smells fantastic. Who knew powdered eggs could smell so good?" She was wrapped in a thick blanket, her wool hat pulled down over her head.

"Herbs can make about anything smell halfway decent." Morgan smiled. "Good morning."

"Hi," Dusty said, finally meeting Morgan's eyes. "How are you feeling? It feels like I ran a marathon yesterday—every muscle is screaming at me."

"Me too."

"We should check with the ranger station to see if they made contact with your family."

"I was thinking the same thing myself," Morgan said. "Hopefully they have been able to reach them. I hate for my parents to worry at their age."

"How old are they?"

"Both are in their mid-seventies." She held her hand up. "Before you ask how old I am, they had me and my sister when they were older."

"How old are you?"

"Don't you know you're not supposed to ask a lady how old she is?"

"You told me to ask you." She laughed.

"I'm thirty-four."

"Thirty-four? Wow, that's young to be the chair of a department at a university. In all of my college book tours, I can honestly say that I have never met someone like you." Dusty cleared her throat.

"Oh? What does a typical chair of a university department look like?" She punctuated *chair* with air quotes.

Visibly flustered, Dusty continued. "Well, someone as young as you and who is the chair of a department. I mean, they are usually, like, older. It's…well…Teggy didn't exactly paint you in a way I was expecting…she said you were her old friend…an old friend…never mind…" She laughed, Morgan joining her. "Well, your parents must be proud. What did they do, for a living? Assuming they are retired, that is."

"They were both professors at Boise State. My father taught engineering and my mother taught German and history. That is probably where I got the idea to get into teaching. You know, what's that saying? About the apple and a tree and falling?"

"Yeah, I know the one. So you are German?" There was an interesting undertone to her query, Morgan thought.

"Yeah, on my mother's side. Why?"

Nothing," said Dusty.

"What?"

"I kind of…when I first met you I thought you might look right at home in a dirndl. "

"A dirndl?" She threw her head back and gave a hearty laugh. Her thoughts shifting from wearing the dirndl to the dirndl being taken off of her by a certain someone. She imagined Dusty pulling at the little string at the top to reveal…

Dusty powered on, fighting a blush. "Well, I am sure your parents are proud of you. You are very good at teaching, judging from what I saw in your classroom and your success with the advocacy campaign and what all Teggy has told me about you." She sat down at the table, which had plates on it piled high with powdered eggs, tomatoes and roasted potatoes. "Yum, thank you. I'm starving."

"That campaign was all my students' doing. I can't take any credit for that. Plus they had a compelling story to inspire them."

"Thank you," she said, filling a fork with scrambled egg. "How did you get into public service?" she asked, deflecting Morgan before she could ask anything personal in return. Morgan gave a mental nod. She would continue to respect Dusty's boundaries.

"My parents are big into community service and giving back. They are probably the only seventy-something Democrats in the state of Idaho. They taught me to constantly ask how my community, my neighbors and those around me could live better. By my senior year of high school, I had a résumé two pages long with community-service projects. Pursuing public service was a natural path for me and I never looked back."

"That's refreshing, being pushed in such a positive direction," said Dusty. "I still remember my first community-service project."

"Oh?"

"Yeah." She chuckled. "Court-ordered after a charge of public indecency—and no, I'm not going to share that story."

"Too bad! Well, then…what about writing? How did you get into it? I mean the subject area, historical fiction?"

Dusty put her fork down, reached for her steaming mug of freeze-dried coffee, and took a sip. "Well, I love history and interconnectedness is something that I've always been drawn to. It is a fascinating part of life that I don't always understand, especially when it comes to decisions that people have made and the ripple effect it creates.

"I am in awe of how one decision, no matter how small, can change the life of so many and can shape history. That is dramatic, I know, but some of the decisions that have been made have had such alarming consequences and life-changing outcomes for millions of others. I always found myself wondering what the world would be like had those decisions taken a different direction. What if the Native Americans never helped those first pilgrims? What if they had left them to die?"

"Interesting," said Morgan. "But what about the line of thinking," she said, unable to resist her natural ability to play devil's advocate as if in the classroom, "that no matter how hard people try to change history, history will always find a way of correcting itself to what we know as actuality?"

"Perhaps, perhaps not." Dusty smiled. "The perhaps-not is where I like to write from. What if the oratory skills that Hitler possessed were directed toward something different— God forbid—another race, for instance, or something totally different?"

"He'd probably be Billy Graham!" said Morgan, causing Dusty to laugh. "It is very interesting to know your mindset with your writing. And I have liked that very thing about your stories, the perhaps-not quality about them. You are truly talented. Your parents must be proud of you too." She spoke with a smile, though it faded quickly when she saw the spark disappear from Dusty's eyes.

"What was it like for you, growing up in Boise?" Dusty asked.

Morgan smiled. She touched Dusty's hand with her own, yearning for Dusty's natural glow to return and seeing it revive. "I am lucky. I had a great childhood and we were a very active family. Camping, traveling and always doing something. My parents are the best, even when I came out of the closet. Of course, I was scared as hell to even talk about it. They knew, though. They would always ask if I was dating anyone and I kept avoiding the question. I never brought boys home. I watched *Xena: Warrior Princess* fifty billion times!" She smiled. "But, yeah, I was scared as hell. I mean, what kid isn't?" She laughed.

"But when I did sit down to tell them, my dad cut me off, saved me from my ramblings and said, 'Morgan, if you are gay, tell us. We will throw you the biggest coming-out party ever.' My whole family has been nothing but supportive of me my entire life."

"Wow, that's refreshing," said Dusty as she got up to take their plates, rinsing them both in a bucket of water. "It sounds like you have a wonderful family. And I totally mean that." She smiled. "So you want to try making contact with the ranger station again to see if they reached your folks?"

"I do, and I should probably get dressed and put my jeans on and something more...cabin-worthy," Morgan said, noting that Dusty had already changed and looked as tidy as could be. "Thank you for washing everything last night and for getting all the firewood and everything. I was exhausted, and those pills and whiskey did me in. I don't even remember falling asleep."

"Well, go ahead. I'm going to bring more firewood from the back. It's starting to rain out there, and by the looks of things," she said, peering out the window, seeing the gray rolling in, "it's picking up. We'll need dry wood to burn. Thank you for making breakfast. I was starving."

"Anytime," said Morgan, meaning it.

* * *

Dusty had taken her time getting as much wood as she could to the enclosed porch. It had been torture at breakfast to sit across from Morgan what with her adorably messy hair and the way she blew at her coffee to cool it down—those lips were driving her mad. When it had become too much for Dusty, she'd decided to channel her…energy into more productive pursuits.

"I got as much of the firewood as I could into the porch, and good thing—it is pouring out there now." Dusty sat on the stone ledge of the fireplace to dry herself off.

"My God, you're soaking wet."

"I'm fine. I'll just dry off here."

"No, you won't. Take your coat off and change your clothes. You're going to get sick. You're making me cold just looking at you."

"Fine," said Dusty as she removed her coat to dry it on the line over the wood stove in the kitchen. She removed her flannel top and added it to the line and pulled out the T-shirt that was tucked into her jeans. Unbuttoning her jeans, she headed to the table where Morgan was sitting and scooped up a handful of dried fruit to eat before heading up to the loft to change. "Did you make contact with the ranger? Hear anything about your family?"

"Yes, I made contact, but she said that she hasn't heard anything back from them yet. She called last night, left a message and also sent them an email, but nothing so far. She said to radio again tomorrow morning. I thought you might like to know. She did get ahold of Tegs. She let her know that you're alive, that you are with me. She said that Tegs sounded really worried about you and said to tell you that she has already updated your contract, though I don't know why she would want to tell you that at a time like this." Morgan sounded perplexed.

"Aww, too funny! Inside joke…kinda," said Dusty. "Any news about the lodge, the workshop people?"

"Yes, she said that the cabins at Bear Creek were hit hard. They were built in the 1920s for logging and converted when the main lodge was built. Some of them weren't really up to code for an earthquake. There've been two casualties among the workshop people, at least so far, one from a heart attack and the other from some poor woman who was crushed in her cabin.

There are sure to be some lawsuits. Maybe lawyers *will* come to the rescue this time." She chuckled, remembering the joke Dusty had told in her class.

"Oh, that's horrible," said Dusty as she descended from the loft clad in her long-sleeve thermal shirt and Uncle Mike's oversized sweatpants. She made her way to the fireplace and sat as close to the fire as possible. She was shivering, but warming up. She looked up, catching Morgan's brief glance at her body, and wondered again how much longer they would be able to hold out.

"But aside from that, most everyone is accounted for from the workshop except for a few other people who were hiking on the trail—they are still looking for them. Needless to say, the workshop has been canceled."

"And Boise? Anything happen in the city?"

"No, nothing, thank God. Most everything affected by the earthquake was concentrated up here. The quake's fault line was here on the mountain. McCall sustained a lot of damage. We're—McCall, that is—all over the national news for the landslides. There were several of them around here. And the reason why they can't spare the air support and a rescue team for us is that a lot of missing and injured people were at Brundage taking advantage of the last few weekends of snow tubing. They are working really hard to get them out in between the storms that keep coming through."

"Wow," said Dusty. "I hope they are okay and not buried alive. How scary, those poor people stuck out there. We are really lucky up here. I mean, to have been so close to your uncle's cabin and to have food and water."

And you, she wanted to add.

CHAPTER TWENTY-ONE

The women spent the rest of the rainy afternoon drinking hot tea, talking shop, and getting to know one another better.

"I really should have been paying more attention. Looking back it was obvious they were going to cut my program."

"How so?"

"All the red tape I had to navigate for the students. It's like whenever we went to the state legislature they had their own dedicated lobbyist to point us in the wrong direction or raise issues. They don't want me to have the resources I need."

"That's crazy, but not unlike what Oregon experienced at the get-go. The good news is that Idaho has one of the more effective Native American tribal coalitions. So you've got that."

"Agreed."

"Actually, that was going to be the premise of my keynote. Lessons learned and ways to collaborate moving forward. In fact…" Dusty got up and looked around. "Paper. I need paper," she said, waving her hands around.

"Check under the board games. Right over there." She motioned to a shelf filled with books and notions.

"Aha. Perfect." She started drawing shapes and circles and writing notes. "You see, I was going to share this." She started linking the shapes together. "A new framework that can work toward shifting the burden of proof from the reservations to bypass the states and route things directly to the federal government."

"That's brilliant." Morgan placed her finger on the sheet of paper. "It puts the offender in a legal limbo of a sort, right? Obligating the feds to intervene."

"Exactly. Your students were not that far from coming up with their own solution. Which, to be quite honest, is the only reason I decided to talk to them. The lawsuit angle, it piqued my interest." She laughed.

"Is that right?"

"Totally. That and I wanted to meet Teggy's 'old' friend." She gave Morgan a smile.

Morgan leaned back, stretching her leg. "To be quite honest, this…" Dusty saw her looking around. "It couldn't have come at a better time. I mean except for the whole being stranded thing."

"It certainly sounds like you had your hands full these past couple of months."

"Full doesn't quite describe it," she lamented. "I was distracted all semester long, trying to balance everything. But working on Tribal Justice, meeting you, it has truly been an honor and made it all worth it."

Dusty looked down and fiddled with the pencil she held in her hand. She looked up with a smile on her face. "The pleasure has been all mine." The look she saw in Morgan's gaze stilled her. "I…I didn't realize what type of reaction *Reservations* would provoke, to be honest. But I had to try."

The look on Morgan's face told her that she too could feel the tension that had transpired. Dusty had put herself out there being honest and forthcoming with information about herself and it took something out of her—not in a bad way but in a different way. A way she couldn't place. She decided to turn the conversation back to safe ground. She talked about her animals, her farm and her travels of late.

She did *not* talk about what she had done after appearances during her book tour, of course—or about what she and Morgan had done prior to the workshop. She was embarrassed at how much she had drank and how many women she had slept with, using them one after another to avoid her emotions. She wondered if any of those women would have been as sweet, as genuine and as funny as Morgan was if she had given any of them the time of day the day after.

They talked until Morgan fell asleep again. Since she was in a seated position with her leg elevated Dusty decided to let her be. She busied herself looking at the old books and magazines on the bookshelf. She also found an album with photos of Morgan. There were photos of her as a small girl, as a young woman and a woman grown. She had always been beautiful. Dusty particularly liked the photo of her when she was about fourteen or so. She wore a crisp white dress, her hair, long and golden, flowed all around her and she was holding a yellow flower. She looked absolutely beautiful and happy.

There were pictures of Morgan's family too, her mom, dad and big sister and another man, her Uncle Mike probably. She saluted the guy for his cabin and great whiskey. She replaced the photo albums and went to the bunker again to get ideas for dinner. Instead of food, however, she got carried away exploring the equipment she found there. There were tools, gadgets, army-issued gear and guns. Most of them were older, but they looked like they would fire if they needed to. There were also several unstrung bows and some arrows. She brought one her size upstairs; she thought she would try it when the weather cleared. She had learned how to use a bow during her time with the Red Elk family, but hadn't shot one since. She wondered if Morgan knew how to use one.

"Really, woman. Were you born in a barn?" Dusty turned next to tidying the small cabin. Morgan had a habit of throwing things hither and thither and letting them lay wherever they landed. She didn't mind picking up after her actually. It helped her keep on point and focused, distracted her from thinking back to the night that they had shared and the kisses and the touches and the taste of her…*Stop*. She commanded of herself.

She shook off the flashback to focus on gathering up some odds and ends. She had acquired the habit of keeping things tidy when she was sent away to boarding school and continued it when she moved in with the Red Elk family, not wanting to be a burden on them. She had done so ever since.

Dusty returned to the porch. As the rain tapered off, warm air had moved in and she heard thunder in the distance. She sat wrapped in a heavy blanket, content to wait for the sun to descend behind the mountains. She hadn't simply sat, doing nothing, in a long time and, despite the trauma of yesterday's events, she had thoroughly enjoyed the sunrises and sunsets she'd witnessed over the past couple of days. She almost felt herself slowly recharging. She wondered if that feeling was what Morgan had meant when she said all she needed to reset her body and soul was to watch a sunrise.

Morgan, now wrapped up as well, joined Dusty with a bottle of wine and two glasses.

"Oh, a merlot!" Dusty said. "This is fancy. Do you think it's still good?"

"There's only one way to find out." Morgan worked the wine bottle open and was rewarded with the healthy pop of the cork.

"That's a good sign."

"Indeed." Morgan stifled a yawn. "Some company! I'm sorry I dozed off again. I guess I needed sleep."

"You don't have to apologize," Dusty said as Morgan filled their glasses. "It's been a strange couple of days." Morgan gave her a glass. They tested it and agreed it was drinkable.

The two sat side by side and enjoyed their wine, finishing half the bottle, Dusty felt content watching the sun go down and listening to the thunder build, the silence between them a comfortable one.

"Thunderstorms are my absolute favorite," said Dusty.

Morgan smiled at her. "You're really enjoying this aren't you?"

"Fuck yeah. Look at the sky." She motioned. "It's stunning. Let me see your watch."

"Sure." Morgan handed it over.

"Got to count the seconds..." Dusty started the timing feature and tallying the seconds between each bolt of lightning and clap of thunder. "Then divide that number by five. That will tell you how many miles away the storm is. A lot of people, they don't know to divide by five."

"Myself included."

"In Seattle thunderstorms are quite rare, you know. There simply isn't very much warm air in the atmosphere to mix with the constant cool rain. Thunderstorms were the only thing I missed from Idaho. Well, that and the sunsets. There are so many damn trees where I live now I can't ever see the sun go down." Her eyes were fixed to the beauty that lay in front of her.

Morgan risked it. "You said that you hadn't been back to Idaho in fifteen years? What happened? What has kept you away from here?" She topped off their glasses with more wine.

Dusty sighed, got up, wrapped in her blanket and stood looking out the screen door.

"It's difficult to talk about," she said.

"No, I'm sorry. I understand, Dusty. It's okay, you don't have to if you don't want to. In fact, it's none of my business. I was curious, that's all."

"I don't even want to *think* about it."

"I totally get it. I shouldn't have asked." She softened her voice. "But you can if you want. You can trust me." Dusty finally looked up to meet Morgan's eyes and genuinely felt that she could be trusted. Morgan had done nothing but make her feel safe since the moment she had fallen into her at the bar.

"I was kicked out of my house when I was a senior in high school."

"What happened?"

"Have you ever heard of Gem State School in Caldwell?"

"Yeah, isn't that like a special school, for kids with emotional issues or something?"

"No," she said, drawing out the *o* in the word. "It's a normal high school. It's a private high school. Rather, a private Christian high school. So as normal as a Christian high school can be."

"Oh, sorry, go on."

"Well, my parents sent me there. I mean, like I had a choice—they are pretty heavy-duty religious." She took a deep breath and continued. "Me and my—well, I guess she was my girlfriend, I had known her since the second grade, and we fell in love and were in love all through high school—we were caught making out. Like I almost had her clothes off, in the band room. We were practically—actually, no, we were having sex." She noticed Morgan's blush. "A couple of religious-nut, perfect-girl fuck-offs, Kelly and Christy, walked in on us. You know the types of girls that go running, blabbing their mouths to whoever will listen. They went straight to the principal and everyone else for that matter and told what they saw."

"Oh, Jesus," said Morgan.

"Yes, the principal would have called Jesus if he could have. Instead he called my parents and her parents and said it was an emergency and they needed to come to the school right away. I thought I was going to die. My parents were livid. They had left work expecting to hear that I'd been hurt or something, only to get there to find out that I had been making out—having sex—with my best friend, another girl. A girl that they had let into their home, had let spend the night hundreds of times."

"You weren't allowed to kiss another girl in high school?" said Morgan, confused. "We had a couple of gay boys at my high school. It wasn't a huge deal to see them making out."

"Did you ever see them in the act?"

"Um no. And I'm not sure what the reaction would have been at our school either."

"Exactly. We weren't only kissing. Even so, that type of behavior, holding hands, kissing, sitting within a close proximity of each other wasn't allowed even if you were straight at our Christian high school. We weren't even allowed to dance." Dusty laughed.

"What? No prom?"

"No, no prom."

"No Homecoming dance?"

Dusty shook her head.

"My parents were furious, embarrassed, shocked. All of the above. I can't describe the anger that I saw in them. Needless to say, we were both suspended for a week though we were allowed to wrap up the school day to collect assignments we would miss. Wasn't that nice? I dreaded going home that afternoon, not sure what to expect. When I got there, they told me that they were sending me to Washington, to a Christian boarding school in Auburn, to finish out my senior year. They sent me off with a single bag of clothes and not much else. Little did they know that on my very first day I'd meet the only out gay boy in the school!" Dusty laughed.

"Jesus, that's horrible."

"When I graduated, they didn't bother to come." The pain she still felt was more noticeable in her voice than she had expected it would be.

"Wow," whispered Morgan. "Have you heard from them since?"

Dusty shook her head. "They didn't come to pick me up at the end of the school year either. I haven't seen them since I left here."

"Dusty, I am so sorry that happened to you." Morgan put her hand on Dusty's arm, rubbing it gently, not caring if she made Dusty feel uncomfortable. She let her hand rest on Dusty's.

Dusty couldn't believe how good it had felt to tell her story to Morgan. She felt like she'd just removed a backpack weighing fifty pounds.

"Of course, you feel bad about being in Idaho again. I feel horrible for prying."

"Don't. You didn't know. It was fifteen years ago." She took a deep breath. "I should be over it by now. But I'm not," she whispered. She looked down at Morgan's hand caressing hers.

She just about died when she felt Morgan lean into her to embrace her and instinctively tensed up. But then she heard Morgan's voice in her head, telling her to let go, and she did. She let herself relax into Morgan as she held her. "Thank you, I...needed that," she said, pulling back breathlessly moments later. Morgan leaned back, smiling at her.

They sat in silence for a moment. Then Morgan said, "Forgive me if this is too much, but have you ever thought—I mean, of course, you probably have, but—have you thought about writing about what happened to you?"

"Actually, I haven't thought about writing about it at all. *Reservations* took a lot out of me. I can't even imagine…"

"You would give voice to a lot of kids who have had similar experiences. You are not the first person I know who has been disowned by their parents because they were gay. There are a lot of young people out there that have had that exact thing happen to them."

"Yeah, I know. I'm not sure I am ready to write about it. Jesus, I can hardly talk about it."

"I know," said Morgan. "When you are ready to talk about it, you could—no, you would—help a lot of people, like you are doing with *Reservations*." She shook her head. "I don't know how you do it."

"Do what?"

"Take the bad that has happened to you and turn it into something good, something positive. You don't see it that way, do you?"

Dusty was at a loss for what to say next. She had never thought about her life in that way. She didn't intentionally mean to spin the bad things that happened to her in a positive way. "No, I guess not. I just wanted to write about what happened to the Red Elks. I wanted people to know, so no one would ever forget."

"So the Red Elks, they were your family, weren't they?"

"Yes, they were. They took me in, not caring where I had come from or who I chose to love. They didn't care what my story was or why my parents didn't want me, because they did. They wanted me in their lives. They took me home to live with them, no questions asked. That first year I was with them I wrote my first three novels—well, the drafts of them. I was so withdrawn. It was horrible. I wrote, rode horses and tried to get through it and move on. They didn't pry, they let me write and be myself. Oh, and my friend Robby. God, I miss him. They saved me from myself, really—from some of the darkest days I have ever known. They were so special to me." Dusty tried to hold her tears back.

"I can't imagine losing my family twice," said Morgan, caressing Dusty's arm again.

"I haven't been back to Idaho since I left for Washington. It's the one place that I have managed to avoid. Well, until now." Dusty stood, dropping her blanket on the little bench below, Morgan's hand slid down her arm to press Dusty's hand ever so gently. The sensation of their fingers intertwining was maddening. She hadn't ever let anyone get this close to her, not ever.

She slowly pulled her hand away. She didn't want to lose the connection they had made, but she didn't dare to take it any further, to feel more. What could come from it? She lived in Washington. Morgan had her whole life in Idaho, a place Dusty wanted to get out of as soon as possible.

Dusty looked down at Morgan, resting her eyes on her mouth, which was just slightly open. Heat rose within her as she remembered the feel of Morgan's lips when she had first kissed her, how incredibly aroused it had made her. She wondered if Morgan knew the effect she was having on her.

"Are you hungry?" Dusty whispered, a clap of thunder breaking their connection. Time to move on.

CHAPTER TWENTY-TWO

Dusty made a dinner of three-bean soup: pinto, kidney and white. She had added some of the barley she had found and a hearty amount of freeze-dried vegetables, using the perfect amount of herbs to pull it all together. She also found wheat flour, salt and oil and made a flatbread for dipping. They ate in silence mostly. The only sounds were of Morgan umming and ahhhing at the tasty dish Dusty had made.

Jesus, everything that Morgan said or did made Dusty want to rip her clothes off and make love to her.

"This is amazing, Dusty. You cook a lot?"

"Yeah, I do. When I am home, that is. I grow most everything I cook at home or get it from the local farmers market. So being here, cooking with what we got, ain't too bad. I am quite enjoying the challenge." Dusty smiled, glad for the small talk. While it had felt good to tell Morgan what had happened to her in high school, it had taken a lot out of her and she was mentally exhausted.

Dusty did the dishes while Morgan rested, then joined Morgan on the couch. In her hands was the bow from the bunker.

"I see you found the weapons," said Morgan.

"Yeah, these are cool. They are pretty high-quality too."

"My uncle gets them from a maker in Oregon, at the Portland Market. They are all custom-built."

"Do you know how to use one?"

"I do. I'm quite good, actually."

"Oh, and modest too?" She laughed.

"I can teach you tomorrow if you like?" said Morgan, blushing at Dusty's comment.

"Oh," said Dusty. "I know how to use a bow. I learned on the rez—you know, from Indians."

"Well, then," Morgan responded, "we should try them tomorrow, have us a little tournament."

"What a great idea," she said, her eyebrows raised. "Care to make it…friendly?" asked Dusty.

"Friendly? Oh, you're on," she said. "What are the terms?"

"Hmm."

"Oh, I know!" said Morgan. "If I win, you have to come back to my class next year and give another presentation."

"Oh, wow," said Dusty, not quite ready for that level of friendliness. She thought for a moment. "I was thinking more like a monetary bet, but okay, sure, why not."

"And if you win?" said Morgan. "How about a bottle of that Johnny Walker?"

"It's a deal. Hopefully it stops raining for an hour or two," she said as she stifled a yawn. "Sorry, I'm not sure why I'm yawning. I didn't really do anything today."

"What time did you wake up?"

"Early. I didn't sleep much. I think I was wired from everything, and I got cold too."

"Why don't you sleep with me?" said Morgan, and then, noting the look of concern in Dusty's eyes, "I mean, sleep next to the fire, with me. I won't touch, I promise. Do you want to? Sleep with me?"

"No, no, that's all right. You should stretch out your leg and elevate it. I'll get myself another blanket or two from the bunker. Besides, I am a light sleeper. I don't want to keep you up with all my tossing and turning." Dusty stifled another yawn.

"No matter what, I can sleep. There could be World War Three going on outside and I would be able to sleep." Morgan smiled.

"Yeah, I have noticed. You sleep pretty darn hard, don't you?" She thought back to making her way out of the house last Saturday. Sneaking hadn't really been required. The woman slept like a log. "If you don't mind and if you don't need anything, I am going to try to get some sleep. Are you good? Do you need anything?"

"No, I'm fine, go on," she said as she stretched, arching her back. Dusty caught herself licking her lips at what she saw. Judging by the look in Morgan's eyes, she had caught that too.

Morgan tried again. "If you do get cold, just come on down. Seriously, there's plenty of room."

"Okay, and if you need anything during the night, just yell for me." Dusty headed to the bunker to get her extra blanket before climbing up to the loft.

"Thanks. Good night, Dusty."

Dusty went to bed, fighting off every urge to take Morgan up on her invitation to join her on the futon. She knew what would happen if she did. She wouldn't be able to let Morgan sleep for at least three days.

Speaking of sleep…it was time to get some rest. She was actually warm this night, thanks to her extra blanket. She listened to Morgan puttering around down in the cabin below, deducing from the sounds that drifted up to the loft that she was fiddling with the archery equipment, looking at books and reminiscing over the old photos. Her last thoughts of Morgan, however, were about being wedged between Morgan's legs, resting her head in her lap, kissing her stomach, making her squirm.

CHAPTER TWENTY-THREE

The two woke up to a beautiful day, blue all around with picturesque puffy white clouds high in the sky.

"No rain for the time being. Great day to try out those bows," said Dusty as she bounded down the ladder from the loft. Morgan was already awake and fidgeting around in the little kitchen.

"Yeah, it's glorious out there. It's only been what, a couple of days up here, but I'm going stir-crazy. I need to get outside and do something, take advantage of the clear skies."

"Yeah, me too."

"My ankle feels a lot better too," Morgan said.

"Great, so then you will have no excuse for when I kick your ass," said Dusty, laughing.

"So much talk. Hey, where are you going?" Morgan asked as Dusty zipped her puffy coat and opened the cabin door.

"Outside. Let's go scope out a place to set up a target."

"Hold on! Not before breakfast. Gotta keep our energy up. I'm starving, aren't you?"

"Yeah, I guess I am."

Morgan heated leftover three-bean stew, mixing in powdered eggs and dehydrated tomatoes. After two cups of freeze-dried coffee, she dressed in her torn jeans, ripped puffy coat, and knit hat while Dusty got everything ready. Dusty had strung two bows, picked out the arrows that were in the best shape and lugged an old, water-soaked and straw-filled target bale out of the remnants of the downed shack out back. She set up the target next to a huge cedar tree near the cabin. She watched Morgan limp to where she'd propped the bows, then went back to the cabin and brought back the bench from the enclosed porch area.

"What's that for?"

"It's for you. No complaints about your ankle, that it hurts. You know it's going to be your excuse for when you are losing, so sit there and rest until it's your turn."

"Please! It feels so much better. And, besides, I could shoot from one leg and probably still beat you." She stood on her good leg and drew the string back in a fairly proficient way to underline her boast.

Looks like she really has shot an arrow a time or two, Dusty thought. *Too bad*. She envisioned herself helping Morgan assume the perfect stance—wrapping herself around her, whispering what to do into her ear, showing her where to position her fingers on the string, just like in the movies. Followed by ending up in the grass, making love, also just like in the movies. She shook her head to clear it.

"So you must have hunted a lot when you came up here on your breaks?" asked Dusty.

"No, not really, my uncle taught us how to use them and we mostly played around with them, shot them into bales of hay mostly. We'd never, you know, hunt with them or anything like Uncle Mike did."

Dusty thought back to the first and only time she had killed anything with the bow. She and Robby had been camping, going two weeks in the mountains with their horses. One day, after leaving their camp for an excursion on their horses, they returned to find all of their stuff gone, missing. Someone had rummaged through their camp, taking all of their food and gear. Luckily they had their horses and their bows. They had no choice but to retreat back down the mountain. Since the journey took a few days, she and Robby had to hunt so they could eat. She was a better shot and had killed a rabbit to sustain them for their trip home. She hated to take the life of another animal. She hated having that much power over something living. She remembered Robby, how sweet he was. She wondered again where he was and how he was doing, if he was still drawing, if he ever thought about her.

Dusty picked up a bow and smiled at Morgan.

"Ready?" whispered Morgan.

"Yeah. You first, or me?"

"Go ahead. Let's see what you got, what you learned on the rez."

"Okay, well, fair warning, these bows are a lot larger than what I would use. I mean, your family is quite a bit taller than me. I found the smallest, lightest weight I could find, but..."

"You haven't even shot the bow and you are already making excuses!" said Morgan, laughing, leaning on her bow.

Dusty stretched her arms and bent over to stretch her legs out. She leaned over to pick some grass and threw it up in the air to see which way the wind was blowing.

"For heaven's sake!" said Morgan, laughing.

"Okay, okay." Dusty chose an arrow and assumed the position. She took a deep breath and let the arrow go. It hit the bull's-eye dead on. She smiled at Morgan. "Yep, still got it."

"You're too close. Back up. Jesus—a child could hit it at that range!"

"What?" Dusty grabbed another arrow and backed up about fifty feet. "Fine!" She assumed the position, let the arrow go and hit the bulls-eye again, dead on. "Aww, hell! I can't see from this far away," she exclaimed. "Did I hit it?"

"Oh my God," said Morgan, "Cocky much?"

"Your turn, at this mark." Dusty used the tip of her boot to reinforce a line in the mud.

"Jesus! Okay, I know where to stand." Morgan found an arrow, assumed the position, shot and sent the arrow past the bale into the ground. "I get another chance! You got two."

"And I hit the bull's-eye both times." Dusty laughed, resting the bow on her crossed arms. "You can scoot up to the child's mark if you need to."

"Oh, please," Morgan said as she hastily got another arrow, strung it up and let it go. She hit one of the outer rings.

She hung her head. "Damn. So you're better than me with this thing."

"What did you say?"

"I said, 'You are better at this than—Destiny!" she said, finally realizing that Dusty had been teasing her.

"You're not bad, though, for having a hurt ankle."

"Yes, the ankle, that's it," Morgan responded. "I think I will take you up on relaxing on the bench."

"You're not giving up already, are you?"

"No, I'm resting, assessing the situation."

She tried for another hour to beat Dusty. She kept her on her toes, but Dusty won each round. It would be fair to say that she had kicked Morgan's ass.

"Come on," she pleaded. "Double or nothing."

"Can you really afford to buy me two bottles of that expensive whiskey?" Dusty teased.

"Are you so sure you are going to win?"

"As much as I would love to make two appearances in your classroom, I'm afraid I just haven't the time." She laughed.

"Come on. You know you want to."

Something in Morgan's tone made Dusty decide to hedge her bet.

"Okay. Okay. In addition to our original bets, how about an extra bottle of whiskey *and* one hundred dollars *if* you can hit the bull's-eye *and* I miss it. What do you say?" Morgan hadn't come close to the bull's-eye yet and she was pretty sure of her own chances even though they'd been at it a while.

"Oh. A parlay. Aren't you sophisticated?"

"You have no idea."

"It's a deal." The two shook on it.

As Dusty reached over to select her favorite arrow, she felt Morgan edge closer to her. She looked at her in time to see her run her hand through her thick blond hair. She flipped it to the side of her shoulder and caressed the arrow in Dusty's hand slightly. "Nice choice of arrow, Destiny. So long, so strong."

"'So long, strong'?" She threw her head back in laughter, Morgan joining her. "Are you trying to distract me, Professor West?"

"Am I succeeding?"

"Not in the least," she said, trying to stop giggling at Morgan's attempt at seduction. She nocked her arrow and shot it. Whether she intended to miss no one would know, but she did and by a lot.

"Don't get too carried away," she said, hearing Morgan's gasp. "You still have to make the bull's-eye," she reminded her. Morgan selected her arrow, pulled back the string and sunk the shaft dead center in the target.

"Just like that." Morgan laughed. "And I don't take checks."

"You hustled me. You totally hustled me."

"It was pure luck."

"I don't think so." She walked over to the bench to take a breather. She decided she didn't mind losing the bet that much. She had missed the feel of the bow in her hands, she realized. Each time she let an arrow go she felt as if she was letting go of a part of her heartache over the deaths of the Red Elks, salving a part of her that she had thought would never heal. Thanks to the playful give-and-take with Morgan, new paths were forming in a deep canyon carved long ago, paths that were changing her association of bows and arrows with the loss of her second family to having fun instead with a new friend.

It made her want Morgan all the more, unfortunately.

They continued to play with the bows until they got hungry. Over trail mix, flatbread and peanut butter, eaten outside in the balmy interlude that had followed the storms, they talked about what they would *rather* be eating for lunch. Pizza topped the list.

Eventually, Morgan got cold and wanted another hot bath. Dusty, on the other hand, declared she was going to spend the rest of the afternoon shooting the bow. Her hands were getting raw, but she didn't think she could go inside and avoid looking at Morgan while she was bathing.

Aside from wanting Morgan's body for her own, Dusty had genuinely enjoyed spending time with her. She was interesting. She also loved that she made Morgan laugh. She thought about the other women that she had slept with and wondered again how much she had lost out on by using them for nothing more than a good time.

When her fingers got too stiff to shoot another arrow, she finally retreated inside the warm cabin. Morgan had dinner waiting for her, and she welcomed it.

CHAPTER TWENTY-FOUR

Following a dinner of MRE ravioli and canned corn, eaten in near silence, the two shared a jar of canned brandied peaches for dessert. It took everything in Dusty's power to not take Morgan's hands into her own and lick the syrup off her fingers and taste the sweet juice on her lips. There were several times where she felt like at any moment she would do just so, especially after their fit of laughter at one of her funnier jokes, something about a genie, champagne and drinking from the bottle—she couldn't remember.

They retreated to the couch with a bottle of wine. Dusty stoked the fire until it shone brilliantly, making their shadows dance joyfully on the cabin walls. Morgan no longer had to elevate her foot; now her feet were stretched out, warming on the fireplace ledge. Dusty sat next to her, her legs crossed.

Morgan broke the silence as always. "Dusty?"

"Hmm," she responded, mesmerized by the dancing firelight. Out of the corner of her eye, she saw Morgan looking intently at her.

"I had fun with you today."

"I did too, Morgan. I haven't actually used a bow in years."

"Oh sure, rub it in, why don't you."

"No, I mean—" She laughed, realizing how she had come across. "I haven't used one since my family—the Red Elks— since living with them. It was fun and I enjoyed it. With you, I mean."

"Me too," said Morgan as she squeezed Dusty's leg briefly, feeling Dusty squirm.

Silence continued as they watched the flickering flames in the fire.

"Dusty?"

"Hmm?"

"Can I ask you something personal, about what happened?"

Dusty shifted in the couch and her heart started to race. "I have told you everything."

"I know, and I am glad you did. Thank you." She shifted, turning her body toward Dusty. "I was wondering what happened to your girlfriend, the one from high school?"

Dusty shifted uncomfortably. "Oh," she said. She hadn't expected that to come up. "I don't really want go into it. Please."

Morgan decided to push for more. It wasn't like Dusty could leave her. It had started raining again, and the cabin was only four hundred square feet in area. Where Dusty would go, Morgan would follow.

"It is important, Dusty. Please, I want to know." She strained to meet Dusty's eyes; she placed her hand on her thigh, nudging it gently. "Please?"

Dusty continued to stare intently into the fire; she ran her hand through her long hair and sighed. She drained her glass and held it out, signaling for Morgan to refill it.

"After we were caught, we only had a couple of moments to talk before our parents arrived. She swore, I swore, that whatever happened, we would tell the truth, we would stand by each other and face whatever criticism, whatever reaction we got from our parents together. Because we loved each other."

She took a hearty swallow of her wine, draining it in one gulp, then, sitting back, she continued.

"When our parents arrived and the principal asked us to explain, Andrea—that was her name, Andrea Fall—she denied everything, said that we were pretending, that I meant nothing to her, it was a joke."

"Wow," whispered Morgan as she broke her gaze away from Dusty's to look into the flames.

"By the time classes were over, the whole school knew what had happened, but they knew it from her point of view. She sided with Kelly and Christy, the girls that walked in on us—playing everything off like it was a joke, that she and I were messing around, that nothing really happened, that we were doing it to piss off one of our teachers. Oh God, and to top it off, everyone kept acting weird around me and the gossip that afternoon was out of control. Leaving the state was almost a relief."

"I bet," said Morgan.

"I think that her lying like she did, was more difficult for me than my parents abandoning me. I had known her since the second grade and started loving her in the eighth grade. I honestly thought that she had loved me too. That she and I were going to go through life together, were going to be one of those stories you hear about: high school sweethearts that stay together through it all." She shook her head. "We had even picked out a college together, applied, been accepted. We had it all planned out."

She sighed. "Maybe it was supposed to happen the way it did, maybe it was better for both of us. I don't know."

"No, I don't think so, Dusty. It may have been better for her in her own mind as a way to justify her being gay, but not for you. You deserved to be loved and to have closure. What she did was—you were betrayed."

"I have never really thought about it that way." Dusty turned to meet Morgan's eyes.

"But weren't there other gay kids at your high school?"

"Not that I knew about. No one really talked about it. I mean, it was a Christian school—it just wasn't talked about; no one was out. I didn't even think of myself as gay. I only knew that I loved her."

"Did she ever try to contact you when you were at the

boarding school?"

"No." She ran her fingers through her hair, then turned back to look at the flames. She hadn't thought about Andrea in years. "I've never told that to anyone before."

"Are you okay?"

Dusty thought for a long time before she finally responded. "Yeah, I am."

"Good. I mean, I am glad. Do you feel any different? Better? You know you can tell me whatever you want, okay?"

"Thanks, Morgan." She paused. "You know what?"

"What?"

"I do feel loads better having told someone. Having told you." She met Morgan's sympathetic eyes. "That was my first experience with love, you know. I'm now realizing that it's what I have been basing my entire love life—or lack thereof—upon. It's a tad pathetic, isn't it? It happened so long ago."

"No. Not at all." Morgan put a comforting hand on her knee.

"I've hurt a lot of women, a lot of people, in my interactions with them, not really caring about their feelings, only protecting myself because…" She fell silent.

"Because you didn't want to be left alone again?"

"I think so," she said in a voice that was not quite a whisper.

* * *

Morgan watched Dusty take a deep breath and struggle to hold back tears. She sat in silence next to her, watching the firelight dance in the room. She understood Dusty a little better now—or thought she did. Understood why she had bolted and avoided her after they had had sex. God, Dusty had had her heart broken and then been forgotten about by her own parents, forgotten by everyone. Her heart had never mended. Morgan didn't think that she would have an easy time of trusting women—trusting anyone—if she had had the same experience.

She patted Dusty's knee again and got up to brush her teeth

and get ready for bed. She must have taken longer than she thought because when she returned, she found Dusty asleep on the futon. She didn't want to disturb her, but she also couldn't climb the ladder to the loft with her ankle in the shape it was in. She had no choice but to join Dusty on the futon, she decided.

She stoked the fireplace with more wood and covered Dusty with a blanket, pausing a moment to take her in, to really look at her. She looked so peaceful. She hadn't seen her look that peaceful and vulnerable before. Her head was turned to the side, and her skin was glowing bronze in the firelight. Her hair, pulled to one side, was lying on her shoulder. The thin T-shirt she was wearing accentuated her full breasts.

Morgan had run her fingers through that hair, had had her mouth on those breasts, had taken Dusty into her body and soul when they had sex. She knew that Dusty didn't—couldn't— want more, but she wondered what it would be like to have her again, whether it would be different a second time and how.

She sat next to Dusty, giving her space, and nodded off.

* * *

Morgan awoke with a start. It was still pitch black outside. The fire had burned down; it looked like an open chest of pirate's gold, emitting a concentrated soft amber glow. She wasn't sure who had pulled who close during the night, or how they were managing to fit on the futon in its upright position, but there they were. She was now lying face-to-face with Dusty, her body pressed so close to hers that she could feel her breasts against hers, could feel her heart beating, her soft breathing on her neck. She ached when Dusty's hold on her tightened and her hand slid to her lower back, coming to rest at her waist. It made her heart feel warm and full. She wondered if Dusty knew what she was doing.

The writer might be embarrassed when she awoke, but Morgan didn't care. She was going to stay where she was. She felt safe in Dusty's arms; she hoped Dusty would feel the same way when she woke up. She stroked hair out of Dusty's face, freezing when she heard her respond with an incoherent whisper before settling back into deeper slumber. Morgan placed her hand on her chest so she could feel her heartbeat, risking the consequences. She'd face those, whatever they would be, in the morning.

CHAPTER TWENTY-FIVE

Morgan was alone when she woke the next morning. *Damn.* She'd been sleeping so soundly she hadn't heard when Dusty got out of bed. She was probably upset with her. Furious.

She should be. She reluctantly shares the most intimate details of her life with me and then wakes up to find me wrapped around her like some kind of...

She couldn't think of a word strong enough to convey how disgusted she was with her behavior. She'd taken advantage of Dusty's vulnerability, resisting dozing off again so she could hold her longer, relishing the feeling of her against her body, committing to memory the way she made her feel. The last thing that had registered before she fell asleep was the early morning light filling the sky—that and the incredible sensation of Dusty's body pressing against hers.

* * *

Christ, thought Dusty, freezing in place as she awoke and realized her body was pressed intimately against Morgan's. Her leg was in between Morgan's, held in place by Morgan's hand, and her head was resting against her chest. This—she didn't do this. She'd never slept—really slept—the night through with another being, another woman, in her life. She'd always left before her partners woke up, Morgan included. But being with Morgan this way felt perfect to her. Felt safe.

And then, suddenly, it felt scary as hell. She gently pulled herself out of Morgan's embrace, fighting the urge to wake her up with kisses and more. It killed her to do so, but she needed some space, some time, to process everything she was feeling. Morgan barely stirred when she left.

When you're good, you're good, Dusty thought ruefully. She was a master at leaving undetected; she had done it so many times before. She threw a couple of logs on the fire for Morgan, then grabbed her water bottle, the bow and some arrows and left. She didn't think she would be able to return to the cabin and face Morgan without wanting to kiss her—without wanting to have her again and again—and that wouldn't be fair to Morgan. Maybe she could shake the feeling with a walk. Maybe when she got back her head would be clearer. She decided to venture down the trail a bit to see if she could see any work being done or if there were any forest rangers around.

She didn't get very far. When she got to the path that they had taken to get up to the cabin, she found it had been totally erased. There must have been another slide. She turned around and hiked toward the small plateau that overlooked the cabin. Breathing deeply, filling her lungs with cold mountain air, she tried like hell to separate her desire for Morgan from what was right. She didn't want to hurt her and going to bed with her again when there was no chance for anything more than sex would do just that. For once, she thought, she was going to do something out of respect for someone else. Or at least she'd try to.

* * *

Morgan understood why Dusty had left. After all, she'd practically mauled her during the night. As much as she wanted to apologize for that, she also sort of hoped when Dusty returned that she would act like nothing had happened.

She fixed breakfast, setting a portion aside for Dusty, and picked at her own. She tried to pass time by reading a book and looking at the photo album, but it wasn't until she finally figured out that one of the bows was gone along with several arrows that she was able to relax a little.

"Good. Good. She likes shooting arrows. If she's doing that, she can't be too upset."

As the noon hour came and went she started to fume. Dusty had been gone more than five hours. "Where the hell is she?"

She lasted two more agonizing hours before she decided—despite her throbbing ankle—that she had to go look for her. She could have fallen or gotten buried by another landslide. She didn't know the land up here as well as she did. It would be Morgan's fault if something had happened to her.

She pulled on her jeans, tied one boot tight and left the one on her healing ankle tied as loosely as possible. She had overdone it at their target tournament yesterday, and it was sore as hell, but she had to risk it. She tucked her oversized flannel top into her jeans, threw her coat on over it and pulled her knit cap down over her ears. It wasn't that cold this time of day, but she didn't want to be walking around unprepared.

Speaking of which, it would probably be smart to bring along some emergency gear too. She dropped some trail mix into Dusty's backpack and was looking around for the first-aid kit when she decided she'd wasted too much time already. "Fuck it!" she yelled, the outburst bleeding off some of the fear that was gripping her. It wouldn't do any good to have Band-aids if she couldn't find Dusty before it got dark. She headed for the door. She decided to look around the lake first. If she wasn't there, she'd take the trail that led to the plateau above the cabin. She headed out.

* * *

"Hey, Morgan. Wow, sure is getting bad out there."

Dusty hung up her coat and shut the door behind her. It had started raining again—pouring, actually—and it was getting windier and colder by the second. She picked up Morgan's watch, which was lying on the counter where she'd put it before taking her bath yesterday.

"Damn!" She was shocked to see how long she had been out. It was going on four, though it was getting dark enough for her to think about lighting the gas lamps. The little bit of sunlight left wasn't strong enough to penetrate the storm passing through.

"Sorry, I didn't realize how long I was gone. I…needed some space. That lower trail, the one we came up on, is totally wiped out." She shivered. It was freezing cold in the cabin. Looking around she saw that there were only ashes in the fireplace and no fire in the wood stove either.

"Morgan? You okay?" She made her way down the narrow hallway, expecting to find her in the bathroom. But the door was open and the room empty. Nor was she in the bunker—the hatch was closed. Or in the loft.

"Shit." Morgan must have gone out, bad ankle and all, to look for her. "Shit, shit, shit."

She put her coat back on, grabbed the wind-up flashlight, and cranked it, noticing as she did the breakfast Morgan had made for her—and the backpack sitting on a chair half-filled. "I'm so sorry, Morgan. So very, very sorry."

She jogged toward the lake, the light of her flashlight bouncing up and down, providing just enough illumination to help her avoid obstacles. "Morgan!" She shined the flashlight toward the lake edge, pointed it into the brush, the trees. Nothing. "Morgan, where are you?"

She turned toward the trail to the plateau where she had spent the day. If Morgan had headed to the path they'd taken to get to the cabin, she'd have seen that it was impassable. The path leading upward would be the only other logical place for her to check.

Dusty trotted up the trail, calling Morgan's name at regular intervals and praying that she'd hear a response. She was able to go at a fairly good pace considering it was nearly dark and with the rain coming down the trail was muddy and slick as hell. She doubled back to the cabin after thirty minutes, hoping to discover Morgan had returned in her absence.

"Morgan? Are you back?" She knew the answer to her question. There was no one home. She took a deep, shaky breath looking around the cabin for clues, as if there would be a neon sign telling her what in the hell she should do. Spotting the radio, she darted toward it, picked up the transmitter and drew a big fat blank. She cursed herself for not paying more attention when they had first used it to call for help. The sweat that she had worked up running around outside turned to a cold and clammy one that was as draining as the turmoil she felt in her heart. She'd be going out again shortly to look for Morgan, but when she returned heat would be helpful. It was something she knew how to do at least. Working as quickly as she could, she stoked the fireplace and stove to a roar and pumped kettles of water to put on to heat upon her return. Vowing that she would not come back until she had found Morgan, she dashed out again into the cold and wet.

When she slipped, tripped and fell fifteen minutes later, she tried to get back up but ended up on her knees again, sobbing. She was a total failure. She and Morgan had made a deal to look out for each other and she had blown it. This was just one more sign that she shouldn't be responsible for another person, another heart, another body. If she found Morgan, she would take care of her, of course—until help came and got them off the bloody mountain. After that, well, she would get as far away from her as possible. That would be the best for everyone concerned.

She pulled herself up and gave another good yell for Morgan. This time she heard a faint yell in response, someone calling her name from farther up the trailhead. As she tried to home in on where it had come from, she heard it again. Morgan had to be close.

* * *

"Over here, Dusty! I'm over here! I'm stuck!"

Morgan was freezing cold and soaked to the skin. She had tripped on a fallen branch and gone over the bank of the trail about twenty minutes into her search for Dusty. How long she'd been there she didn't know. In the process of trying to get back on the path she'd injured her ankle further. She must have passed out, she decided, judging from how dark it had become and the rain that was pelting down. She'd come to just before she heard Dusty yelling for her.

"God, what a fucking idiot I am," she whispered. She had been out on these trails her whole life, but in her quest to find Dusty she had been careless, possibly fatally so. She shivered and called out again to Dusty.

* * *

"Down here, Dusty. On the left side of the trail. I'm down here!"

Dusty shone the light down the edge of the trail bank, trying to make out shapes behind the tall ferns and little evergreens. Finally, she spotted Morgan, stuck between a rock and a large tree. She looked so helpless.

"Oh, Morgan! Are you all right? Jesus, I am so sorry. Are you hurt? Of course you're hurt or you would have… Oh, God."

She took a deep breath. "I am going to get you out of there. Hold on." Dusty shoved the flashlight in her coat pocket and eased herself carefully down the bank. While it was not that steep, it was a muddy and slippery mess. It wouldn't do for both of them to be hurt. Reaching leveler ground, she pushed through the branches and shrubbery until she reached Morgan.

"I am so sorry!"

"No, it's not your fault. I am so stupid for coming out here. I thought maybe you were hurt. I—I wanted to make sure that you were okay." Morgan's teeth chattered as she spoke.

"Shh, it's fine. It was my fault. I lost track of time. I'm sorry for making you worry. Hang tight. Oh, sweetheart..." Dusty moved Morgan's wet hair out of her face, stroking it with her hands, noticing as she did that she had scrapes there and was as cold as ice.

"Jesus, you're freezing." She grabbed her into her arms, holding her close. "How long have you been down here? I must have walked right by you twice now."

"Falling down here was about the first thing I did. I got too close to the edge and tripped on a fallen branch."

"Didn't you hear me walk by? I was just up the road there."

"After I slipped down the side, I tried to climb my way out—so fucking stupid—and I fell again. My ankle is really fucked up now. I think I passed out from the pain. I woke up just before I heard you yelling."

"Come on," said Dusty. "Let's get out of here. Wrap your arms around my neck. We'll stand up together."

"I can't," Morgan said, moaning in pain as Dusty tried to move her.

"You can. You need to try."

"Oh, fuck!" Morgan wrapped her arms around Dusty's neck, whimpering as she realized how weak her body was. Dusty held her around her waist, pulling her close as she lifted.

"I got you," she said. "I won't let you fall again, I promise."

"Jesus. I hope to God it's not broken. I'm so fucking stupid. I'm sorry, this is all my fault. You felt so good last night. I'm sorry I made you feel uncomfortable. I woke up and you were there and I took advantage of you and..." She started crying, unable to say any more.

"Hey, hey, it's okay," said Dusty as she clasped Morgan to her body, trying to warm her. *You felt so very good too*, she thought. "I'm the one that left and made you worry. I was childish for running out like that. But it's going to be just fine. None of that matters now. We're going back to the cabin."

Dusty used her flashlight to scan the rain-swept terrain. "There's no way we can make it back up that bank. We're going to have to follow this slope down until it evens out. Hold on to me." Morgan leaned on Dusty as they bushwhacked their way back toward the cabin.

It had taken her a quarter of an hour to get from the cabin to this point on the trail, Dusty figured. Given the rough terrain they were traversing now and Morgan's injuries, it was probably going to take at least an hour to get back to the cabin and dry clothes. If they were lucky.

CHAPTER TWENTY-SIX

It was actually more like two hours before they got back. Dusty helped Morgan make the last few steps into the screened-off porch and sat her down on the little bench, where she flopped back against the wall, eyes closed.

"Sit tight." Dusty quickly hung up her wet coat and took off her muddied boots and wet socks. "I'm going to put the kettles on to heat for a bath. I promise you it's nice and warm in there. I will be right back."

"Umm hum," groaned Morgan.

Pleased at herself for thinking to get the fires going earlier, she placed the kettles on the stove, then returned to Morgan. "Hey, how you doin'?"

"I'm more cold than anything, which is good, I guess, because I can't feel any pain yet."

"I know, sweetie. Let's get that coat and those boots off. Are you ready?"

"Yes. Just go slow."

"Yeah, nice and slow," said Dusty. Though she was as gentle as possible, there was no way to get the boot off the injured ankle without causing some pain.

"Oh, fuck," Morgan said, moaning and writhing.

Dusty rubbed Morgan's thigh. "Let's go inside to get the rest of your clothes off. Come on now," she whispered. "Up, let's get you inside."

Morgan wrapped her arms around Dusty's neck again, and Dusty lifted her up and helped her inside. She might not be in the same good shape Morgan was—or she had been—but she was strong. Good thing too. She had practically had to carry her the entire crawl back to the cabin.

Dusty grabbed a chair from the dining table. "Sit here. Let's get your wet clothes off and put you by the fire on the couch, take a look at your ankle and then get you into some hot water."

"Sounds like a plan," said Morgan. She closed her eyes as she slowly untucked her flannel shirt, undid the buttons and let it drop soddenly to the floor. Next she peeled off the thin T-shirt she'd been wearing under it, revealing that she hadn't been wearing a bra. Morgan must have thrown her clothes on in haste as she prepared to look for her, Dusty realized with a pang, otherwise she would have been wearing additional layers. Yet another reason to feel bad for leaving as she had.

Morgan sat back in the chair to remove her jeans. Knowing she'd need some help getting them off, Dusty moved closer. At this distance, the firelight revealed new scratches on Morgan's chest and hands. Instinctively, she reached out to touch the deeper ones, the ones on her chest.

"You poor baby." She lightly touched the area around the abrasions, removing her fingers quickly when she felt Morgan's breathing stutter in response.

"Can you help with my jeans?" Morgan asked softly. "I can manage the zipper, but my fingers are too stiff to pull them off."

"Of course." Dusty studied the situation. "Probably best if you stand up, huh?" When Morgan nodded, she helped her up, feeling Morgan's breasts brush against hers as she lifted. When Morgan was upright and holding on to the chair for balance, she peeled the wet fabric down, exposing her beautiful long legs, which were blue with cold. She had her sit back down then and got on her knees to help her ease the pants the rest of the way off, taking special care with the foot that was injured.

"Come on. Let's start getting you warmed up." Dusty layered blankets and towels on the couch for Morgan to sit on, then helped her over to it, wrapping the softest blanket around her.

"Here." She handed Morgan two painkillers and a glass of whiskey to wash them down. "Swallow these. They shouldn't take long to kick in."

"Why, Dusty, first you take my clothes off and now you're trying to get me drunk?" Morgan said, a chuckle in her voice.

"Any chance I get to remove your clothes, I'll jump on it," Dusty said, relaxed enough now to take whatever Morgan threw at her and give it right back. "As a matter of fact, I'm going for your socks next."

She sat on the fireplace ledge, gently taking Morgan's foot into her lap. "Let's see what we have here." As she lifted Morgan's leg, the blanket parted, revealing everything up to her wet panties and triggering thoughts of the last time she was between those legs. She swallowed hard, cursing herself for thinking about that at a time like this and then cursing herself again as she remembered that Morgan was in pain.

"Shit," she said as she gently poked the fat ankle in her hands. She reached for the scissors in the first-aid kit she'd set on the hearth and carefully cut off the sock. "Can you move it? Don't try if it hurts too much."

"Yeah, I can move it. Barely. But—damn!—it hurts," Morgan said through gritted teeth. "Uh," she groaned. "I probably tore a ligament or something." She threw her head back, resting it on the top of the couch. The blanket shifted again as she did, revealing her smooth shoulders, the tops of her breasts and her tight stomach.

Dusty licked her lips, mesmerized by the beauty in front of her. Her eyes followed her tight legs up to her stomach, rested for a moment at the top of her breasts, moved to her long neck—exposed—and finally rested on her mouth. Tearing her gaze away before Morgan could catch her looking, Dusty gently put her foot down and rose to tend to the water. "Drink that whiskey. The water is just about ready for you."

As she tested the temperature of the water, Dusty made a mental list of what she needed to do next. She would tend to her own needs, she decided, get on some dry clothes of her own, once she had made Morgan something hot to eat and put her to bed. First, though, a bath to warm her up. "Are you ready?"

"Yeah." Morgan shrugged off the blanket and reached a hand out to Dusty. She helped her get up from the couch, trying—unsuccessfully for the most part—to keep her eyes off her slender figure, tight abs, perfect long legs and those incredible full, heavy breasts.

"Thank you," Morgan said slowly. Placing one hand on Dusty's shoulder for balance, she used the other to strip her panties down and step out of them, standing fully nude in front of Dusty, who was trying hard not to hyperventilate. "Can you help me into the tub?"

"Of course."

Morgan put her weight on her good leg and let Dusty brace her as she lifted her hurt ankle into the tub. She lowered herself into it and sighed. "Oh," she moaned. "This feels good, Dusty, so good. I was so cold out there and…" She took a shaky breath. "So scared that you had…that you were hurt." She opened teary eyes to meet Dusty's, then closed them and ducked her head, looking disconcerted.

"I was afraid a bear had gotten you," replied Dusty, looking to ease her discomfort.

"A bear?" chuckled Morgan.

"Yeah, you said there were bears here and I thought—" She took a deep breath, deciding a little truth wouldn't hurt. "I was worried about you too." *I was afraid I had lost you*, she thought. "I am so sorry, Morgan, so sorry." Dusty softly stroked the hand Morgan was resting on the edge of the tub, avoiding the scratch etched across her knuckles. "Try to relax. That was then, this is now. Everything's going to be okay."

Dusty drew a chair closer to the tub and sat down, warming herself in the heat of the wood stove and monitoring Morgan.

Watching the color start to return to her cheeks, seeing how her skin glowed in the firelight, noting the way her breasts peeked out of the water every time she inhaled. She looked like a Greek goddess in a bathhouse, steam rising up all around her.

Dusty hesitated for a moment, then, as if in a trance, she grabbed a small towel, dipped it in the water and began to wipe Morgan's face, gently removing dirt and debris from the scratches and scrapes there. She submerged the towel in the water and squeezed it over Morgan's head to get at the mud and the little bits of twig tangled in it, instinctively whispering soothing words to her as she did. As she helped wash her. Helped take care of her.

* * *

Morgan touched Dusty's hand with her own, breaking her out of the trance she seemed to have fallen into. "I don't see why you were so scared of taking care of me, Dusty—you could practically be a nurse. Thank you." She pulled Dusty's hand to her heart and held it there, meeting Dusty's gaze, then sighing and closing her eyes.

Despite being hurt and in pain, Morgan wanted Dusty, wanted her badly. She wanted to be held, wanted Dusty to make love to her, to feel her kisses on her mouth and her body. Her heart sank. It could never happen. Dusty had a life in another state. And she had made it very clear that she didn't want anything more from her. She let go of Dusty's hand.

Her heart skipped a beat when Dusty took her hand again and kissed her palm gently. Cupping Morgan's face in her hand, she stroked her cheek with her thumb. Then, looking resolute, she removed her hand and stood up from her chair. "I am going to make you something to eat and then put you to bed. It's been a long day."

Morgan nodded, trying to hide her regret. *It is what it is*, she thought. *No point in trying to make more of it.*

After Dusty made them a hot dinner—a dehydrated soup mix accompanied by more whiskey—she helped Morgan dress in one of her uncle's flannel shirts and flannel boxer shorts. She helped Morgan settle in on the futon and taped up her ankle to keep it stable.

"Are you still awake?"

Morgan opened her eyes. She'd closed them to concentrate on how nice Dusty's touch felt on her ankle. "Aside from feeling like a complete idiot, I am fine: warm, a little buzzed. I'll live, thanks to you," she said with a smile.

"Thanks to me? You could have died out there!" Dusty hung her head. "You should be livid with me for making you worry. I don't blame you if you don't trust me ever again."

"I don't blame you, Dusty. It was stupid of me to run out there like that to look for you. I should have trusted that you would be okay."

"I hurt you."

"No, you didn't. I had an accident. I was careless out there, not you." She tried to sit back up. Dusty had to practically force her back down.

"Do you need anything before I head to the loft? Do you need more water? Did you get enough to eat?" she said.

"Yes, I am fine, really. But, Dusty?"

"Hmm?"

"Thank you. I don't know how to thank you. I was—it was really scary there for a while."

Dusty shook her head. "The only thanks I need is you being here and okay. Try to get some rest. We have at most only a day or two more out here and then you can have real food and get that ankle looked at. You will be fine. Yell if you need anything."

"I will," Morgan promised with a smile, closing her eyes. "I'll warn you, though, I can be quite demanding when I am hurt."

CHAPTER TWENTY-SEVEN

Crazy thoughts raced through Dusty's head as she tried to get to sleep.

She'd spent hours earlier in the day sitting and pacing around outside, trying to avoid feelings that were starting to consume her and eventually deciding that she wasn't capable of anything long term—*Hell, of anything longer than one night!*

She'd returned to the cabin determined to leave town as soon as they were rescued. Morgan would be better off without her—and vice versa. Then she'd discovered Morgan was gone. And totally freaked out. And spent the evening tending to her ankle, helping her bathe, fixing her dinner.

She had never taken care of someone like she had just taken care of Morgan.

Which was only right, considering she was entirely to blame for what had happened. Which proved again that she wasn't cut out for...for whatever this was. Didn't deserve it.

She closed her eyes, wishing again that she had stayed to wake up with Morgan this morning. As she was about to drift off, however, she heard Morgan whimpering softly and tossing about in the bed below.

Dusty descended the ladder. Morgan was dreaming. Dusty sat down beside her and placed her hand on her chest to soothe her and wake her up.

"Morgan, hey, shh-shh. Wake up. You're having a bad dream. Wake up." The words came out of her, foreign-sounding, as she comforted her patient. "Hey, it's me, wake up."

Morgan awoke with a start. She was sweating. Dusty freed her from the blankets she'd gotten tangled in and pulled down the flannel top bunched up under her breasts. Her skin was hot under her touch.

"Morgan, you're burning up." She reached for the glass of water next to the futon and two of the fever reducers from the first-aid kit. She placed them in Morgan's hands, urging her to take a drink.

Struggling to control her breathing, Morgan sat up. "Thank you," she said in between gulps of water. "I don't feel sick. I think I just had a bad dream—the landslide, falling. I am fine, though. I just need—I'm fine." She took another big gulp of water.

"You scared me," said Dusty, brushing Morgan's hair from her face and tucking it behind her ears.

"I'm sorry. I didn't mean to. It was a bad dream."

I'd give anything to take away the pain, Morgan, to take care of...

Dusty tried to look away from Morgan's intense eyes but found she couldn't. Overwhelmed with feelings she had never known, she couldn't control herself. She caressed Morgan's cheek, tracing her lips with her thumb and pulling them apart. Morgan's eyes closed at her touch. Hers closed too, but popped open again when Morgan's hand grasped her shirt collar, pulled her close, and leaned in to place a kiss on her lips, the sweetest kiss she had ever felt.

Dusty gasped, her heart completely stolen away. She opened her mouth and gently traced Morgan's lips with her tongue, her heart skipping a beat when she felt Morgan's tongue meeting her own. They tasted each other for a moment. Moaning and trembling from being touched so deeply, Dusty could hardly breathe. She was on the edge of a steep cliff; Morgan's kisses would save her from falling or they would push her over. It was life or death.

Morgan gently pulled Dusty down on top of her, all the while continuing the soft exploration of her lips. Their kisses were different this time—no longer the rush job of raw and utter need they had experienced their first time. This time it was an exploration of each other, a question-and-answer session.

With her kisses, Morgan asked Dusty why she was so scared. Dusty's kisses said she didn't know why, but she felt less scared when she was with her, in her arms. Dusty, in turn, asked Morgan if she would ever deny that her love for her was real. Morgan's response was simple; with her kisses she said, "Never." She would never deny her anything, whatever she wanted she could have. Morgan said that Dusty could have her heart if she wanted it.

Their breathing grew more ragged, threatening to eclipse the crackling of the fire, the gusts of wind buffeting the small cabin, the pattering of rain on the roof, and their bodies began aching with a longing for each other. A longing that Dusty had had since the moment she left Morgan's house and that Morgan had had from the moment she awoke alone the morning after they had met.

"Morgan," said Dusty, feeling Morgan's arms make their way underneath her nightshirt, almost pulling it off her body. "Morgan, we can't." Dusty pulled herself away from Morgan's intoxicating kisses. She looked into her eyes. She wanted to take everything the woman was willing to give her and then some, but she couldn't let that happen. "We can't."

"No, I know we can't." But she continued to give Dusty gentle kisses, stoking the fire within her. Their kisses once again grew ravenous and desperate. "It's just…you, you feel so good."

"You feel good too," said Dusty between kisses. "But I don't want to hurt you." She said with a little more edge to it as Morgan's grip tightened. She tried like hell, but she couldn't resist letting her leg press gently against Morgan's center.

Morgan's moan of pleasure at the contact was almost too much, but, gathering her resolve, she shifted the leg to safer territory. She sat back up, pulling Morgan up with her.

"I've got to take care of you now; I can't hurt you anymore." She held Morgan's hands in her own, pressed her forehead against the blonde's.

"I was so scared, Dusty," said Morgan. "So scared out there."

"I was too. When I couldn't find you, I almost lost hope." She wrapped her arms around Morgan. "I don't know what I'd have done if…"

"Thank you for finding me." Morgan straddled Dusty's leg. "Thank you for finding me." She peppered tiny kisses on Dusty's neck. "Thank you," she whispered into her ear.

Dusty held her tight and groaned as Morgan began rocking gently on her thigh, pressing herself on her, slowly, and moaning as she moved herself up and down on Dusty's leg. Dusty held her in place, her hands shaking.

"Morgan, I'm so glad I found you." She tightened her embrace. "So very glad I found you."

It took every bit of self-control she had, but Dusty held herself back. It would be so easy to move Morgan's boxer shorts over a quarter of an inch. That's all that would be needed to feel Morgan on her fingers, to slide inside her and give her what she so clearly needed.

"You feel good, incredibly good, but I…I've got to take care of you. You're hurt." She could feel Morgan's wetness on her leg through her boxers. "Morgan, we can't. Please, I can't."

Finally, Morgan drew her lips from Dusty's and rested her head on her shoulder. "I'm sorry." Dusty looked down, feeling a faint wetness on her neck. The tears she saw on Morgan's cheeks broke her heart.

She pulled her closer. "Oh, Morgan, you had a bad day and I hurt you. I don't want to hurt you anymore. I want to make you safe."

Morgan groaned. "I do feel safe, with you."

"You do?"

"Yes, your kisses, they make me feel safe."

"They do?"

"Yes." Morgan pulled back to look into Dusty's eyes, then at her lips. "Please, can I have one more? Just one more kiss?" Without waiting for an answer, she began kissing Dusty on the neck, on the chin and finally the lips again.

Dusty relented. "One more kiss and then we sleep, okay? Just...one...more." Her eyes closed, her heart pounded. Her center ached.

After pushing her onto her back, Morgan slowly pulled off the flannel top she was wearing, revealing her perfect, full breasts. Dusty wanted nothing more than to take them into her hands, to make her squirm, to reduce her to a panting mess that only she, herself, would be able to put back together. Her fingers, moving on their own accord, lightly touched Morgan's stomach, then brushed over Morgan's nipple, which tightened instantly.

"Morgan, do you have any idea what you do to me?"

"Tell me?" Morgan said, shifting her golden hair to the side with a flip of her head. She worked Dusty's legs open with her knee and pushed her top up so their breasts would rub against each other when she lay on top of her.

Dusty lost all control. She pulled Morgan hard onto herself, reached down to her legs and slipped her hands up and under her flannel boxers to grab on to her backside. She held her hips tight and ground into her, getting a whimper of pain in response.

Morgan jerked up. "Ah!" She pulled up sharply off Dusty.

"Did I hurt you? I did, didn't I? Jesus, I'm so sorry."

"I'm fine. My ribs, they hurt, and I hit my ankle on something. Damn it." Morgan managed to get the words out in short clipped breaths while still sitting atop Dusty. "I'm sorry, you're right. This was a stupid idea."

She patted her chest, trying to calm down. When her breathing evened out, she reached around, found her shirt, put it on and slowly got off Dusty, making her way to the side of the bed. She sat on the edge with her head in her hands.

"I can't help myself with you. That was selfish of me. I took advantage of you, just like I did last night. I needed you, and the worst part of it is I know you don't need—don't want—any of this."

"It's my fault, I started it. I couldn't help myself either. I just—I don't want to hurt you," Dusty whispered.

"You won't hurt me," Morgan said. "You won't."

"But I might," she whispered. She had finally connected with someone. Morgan had reached inside her, had made her say things, share things about herself, and it felt good. Amazing. She wanted this woman, again and again, over and over, every day.

At the same time, it was obvious to her that Morgan wanted more from her than she could give. For one thing, Morgan's work, her family, everything was centered in Idaho, and she had absolutely no intention of returning to live here. As for the rest, whether what they had would last...well, it seemed inevitable to her that she would hurt Morgan emotionally at some point. Better sooner rather than later. She wanted to go home and forget everything that had happened, but she wasn't sure she could.

Dusty sat back up. It pained her to sit—her center was swollen and aching, in need of release. She put her hand on Morgan's back, rubbing it in slow circles. She wrapped her arm around her, caressing her gently on her chest and stomach.

"I am sorry I hurt your ribs."

"It's okay," whispered Morgan.

"Come on, lie back down with me. I'll sleep with you tonight."

Morgan took a deep breath and nodded. Dusty pulled her down onto her back, rolled her onto her side and wrapped her arms around her, holding her close and tight. She whispered things to her, soothing her until her breathing returned to normal. Until her own breathing evened out.

She tried to stay awake, to savor every moment. She had the sense Morgan was trying to do the same. Eventually they succumbed to sleep, their breathing in sync with one another.

What the hell is going on here? Dusty thought as she drifted off. *And what the hell am I going to do about it?*

CHAPTER TWENTY-EIGHT

Dusty woke to the sounds of birds chattering, a sliver of sun peeking into the cabin between the curtains and a beautiful woman lying next to her. The storm had passed and they had weathered it, both physically and, for the most part, emotionally.

Dusty took a moment to survey the beauty sleeping next to her. Morgan's hand was resting on Dusty's chest, directly over her heart. She covered it with her own, trying to savor the moment, anticipating what she was going to say to her when she woke up. The thought scared and excited her.

Needing to feel more of her, Dusty placed gentle kisses on Morgan's lips to wake her up. Finally, Morgan, eyes still closed, opened her mouth to brush Dusty's lips with her own, tracing her bottom lip with her tongue. Their kisses continued that way, soft and tender, until Morgan awoke fully, with a start, her eyes opening wide. She sat up, almost dumping Dusty onto the floor.

"Shit, Dusty. Christ," she stammered.

"What? Morgan, what?"

"Oh my God, last night, I'm so embarrassed—throwing myself on you like that."

"No, it's okay. Please. Don't be embarrassed," said Dusty, smiling.

"You just felt so good." Morgan put her hand on her forehead, rubbing at an ache there.

"You felt good to me too." Dusty took Morgan's hand into her own. "How do you feel today?"

"I'm fine," she said, though her cry of pain as Dusty pulled her to a sitting position told another story. "I need to go, though. You got to let me go."

Dusty's heart sank. "What? Why?"

"I need to use the bathroom—all that water I drank last night."

"Oh," laughed Dusty. "Sure, of course," she said with relief. She pulled Morgan up onto her feet, bracing her as she was a little wobbly, and helped her hobble to the bathroom.

"I'll add some logs and get the wood stove going. Do you want coffee?"

"Oh, yes, please!" Morgan yelled from the bathroom. "Coffee, even freeze-dried, sounds heavenly."

Dusty slipped on her long wool socks and pulled oversized sweats on over her flannel boxer shorts. She stoked the fireplace and the wood stove to a loud roar. Her thoughts were primarily on the warmth inside her that came from Morgan. But her old ways of thought were tugging at her too. What could come of this? Nothing really. She lived in Washington, she had her farm and her animals. Morgan had her program at the university. In Idaho.

The more she thought about what she was going to say, the more she dreaded it.

"I'll tell you what I am really looking forward to." Morgan slowly returned from the bathroom, using the wall to brace herself. "A wet cappuccino from Moxie Java."

Dusty went to meet Morgan and help her the rest of the way down the hall. "You know what I miss?" she said.

"What?"

"Fruit."

"Clean socks!"

"My horses!" Dusty gently placed Morgan in the chair. "I miss pizza. Oh God, what I wouldn't give for a slice of pizza."

"Cold beer!" they said in unison, laughing together.

Their smiles faded and eyes stared intently at each other.

"I think I want to try the ranger station before we have breakfast," Morgan said. "I hope they were able to contact my parents. In all the craziness yesterday, I never called to check in with them. I hope they don't think we got in trouble or anything."

"Sounds like a plan. I'll get the radio. Let me get the water going for your coffee," Dusty said.

She was turning to the window to part the curtains to let more light into the cabin when she heard it. Her heart sank. "Hey, Morgan," she said, keeping her gaze fixed out the window so Morgan couldn't see her expression. "I don't think you will need to call the ranger station today."

"Why not? What do you mean?" Morgan said. "Oh," she said, a note of dismay in her voice. She must have heard the sound of approaching engines then too.

"The rangers are here. They have four-wheelers. We're... being rescued." Dusty turned to look at Morgan, wondering if her eyes looked as sad as Morgan's did. What she wouldn't give for just one more day with her.

CHAPTER TWENTY-NINE

"Please, please, I am short a girl again."

"You need to hire someone," said Morgan, taking a sip of the fresh Long Island Iced Tea that Rosalie had set before her.

"I know," said Rosalie. "I really do need to hire someone. But, until then, can you please, pretty please, help me out Saturday, week after next, for ladies' night? Come on, this isn't another one of my ploys to keep an eye on you. I really need your help and would love even more to hang out."

Morgan had returned from the cabin mostly unharmed, though she had needed a month and a half of almost daily physical therapy to strengthen her torn ligament. It was healing nicely, but she was in pain on the inside. She hadn't yet talked about her time on the mountain with Dusty, but Rosalie had figured out that something big had happened and was trying her best to get her to discuss it or, barring that, to distract her. "Come on, it'll be fun. Like always."

"You know I would love to, but I won't be any use to you. I can't move very fast on my feet. My ankle still bothers me a lot.

I've got to take it easy." Morgan looked at her foot, bobbing it up and down. "It's bad enough I haven't been able to fit into any of my heels. I have to wear these ugly clogs everywhere."

"Oh, they're not that bad."

"Uh, yeah, they are," she said. Her eyebrows were raised in faux amusement.

"Yeah," said Rosalie, trying not to laugh. "I guess they are. Listen, I already thought about your clogs. I was going to ask Sergio to tend with me and you can take his spot as bouncer."

"Bouncer? What if someone gets out of hand? I can't run that fast in these things."

"Oh, please. Since when have we ever had to run someone down?"

Morgan dropped her eyes to her drink, remembering how she had practically sprinted after Dusty when she had left her coat the night they had met.

"Just sit on the little stool, check IDs, stamp their wrists, show some cleavage. You'd be helpin' a sister out big-time, and it comes with free iced teas all night long. It would mean the world to me," Rosalie said. "And, after, we can have a late dinner—or early breakfast—and talk. Okay? I want you to stay over too. We'll have a slumber party." Rosalie's hands clasped together as if she were praying.

Morgan took a deep breath and relented. She couldn't say no to her best friend, and she needed to get out of the house to take her mind off Dusty. She had dominated nearly every waking hour of her life during the two and a half months she had been home. Everywhere she looked she was reminded of her. The Caldwell Night Rodeo. The rain. The smell of cedar trees. Sunrises. And sunsets. And, of course, the continuing work on the Tribal Advocacy Campaign.

"Fine. I'll do it. Only because I love you and you need me. You don't have to pray to me." Morgan waved her hand as if shooing away a fly. "The begging is good enough."

"Thank you," said Rosalie, taking Morgan's hand in her own and rubbing it gently. "Morgan, I'm here for you whenever you're ready to talk about it, okay?" Their tender moment was cut short as Rosalie was called down to the bar to wait on a handful of girls.

"I know you are, and thank you," Morgan said, eyeing the girls. "Go. It's all right."

Morgan continued working on her Long Island, the third of the night. She couldn't feel its effects; she was too numb. She stirred the ice around. She loved to hang out with Rosalie. Even when she wasn't working. She craved the club scene and the loud music. But the club was where it had all started, where she had met Dusty. Another harsh reminder.

She had tried to stay away from the place, but she couldn't help it. She dropped by regularly, spending more time drinking there than she would have liked. She was hoping, she realized, that at any moment Dusty would return to her. She never did, though, which only made things worse. She had been crazy to think anything could happen between them. But she couldn't deny her feelings: she had fallen in love with Dusty in those three days at the cabin. She had fallen in love with the sad girl who, with each passing day, had seemed to grow more and more at peace, more grounded. Dusty desperately needed to be loved and Morgan desperately wanted to be the one to love her fully and without condition.

She thought that, maybe, Dusty had felt something too. She had made it clear to Morgan from the get-go that she didn't want anything more than a physical relationship, a one-night stand. But it felt like that changed the day she had reinjured her ankle. Remembering now what she'd felt then almost stilled Morgan's heart.

They kissed a lot that night, but they didn't end up making love. What they did was far more intimate. They took turns touching each other, feeling each other's bodies slowly and deliberately. They took turns exploring each other, the softness of their skin, the silkiness of their hair. Childhood scars were touched tenderly, hands held and legs and arms caressed.

Her memories of coming down the mountain, on the other hand, were a painful blur. They had taken separate four-wheelers down. Dusty rode with the ranger. Morgan rode a larger four-wheeler with the EMT. Her four-wheeler had to go slow, stopping several times for her to rest and recover from the intense pain caused by crossing the rough terrain. Even with the heavy-duty wrap the EMT had applied on her ankle it was excruciating at times. It was late afternoon by the time she finally reached the bottom.

By the time she got back to the lodge, Dusty had already left. She hadn't heard from her since. The more she thought about everything, the clearer it all was. The fiery kiss they shared before getting on the four-wheelers—it had been a good-bye kiss, not a see-you-at-the bottom kiss.

Sometimes when she thought about it she got really angry. That never lasted long though. It was usually followed by feeling sad about being left, forgotten, brushed aside. Why would Dusty do that to her after she had told her about her own experience of being left and forgotten? Then again, why would Dusty wait for her? It's not like they went up there together as lovers. They hadn't even been friends. She tried to give her the benefit of the doubt. Maybe she didn't realize that her actions were causing others to feel the way she had felt when she was abandoned by her family and her girlfriend.

Hoping word might get to Dusty and trigger some kind of response, she sent an email to Teggy, asking if Dusty was okay and recovering from her ordeal in the mountain. She received a note in return saying that Dusty was doing fine, thank you for taking care of her, let's catch up when you're in Seattle. Morgan didn't press. Dusty knew how to reach her if she wanted to.

The first month back was the hardest, though work and her therapy helped to distract her from thinking about her time in the cabin. She also received a pleasant surprise: her program was going to receive a large grant that would allow her to expand it and get an important accreditation. She had worked hard to write the grant application in the months prior to the workshop—and would have to work even harder to bring her proposed plans to fruition.

She shook her head. As it was, she already felt she wasn't giving her students and faculty all they needed, and it was only going to get worse. Her students and program were her entirety. They had been anyway. Work didn't seem now like it should take center stage anymore, not when there were other things, other people, family, that could make her happy.

She would call Alex from the Art Department, Morgan decided. She had to know if her feeling for Dusty was merely lust, something due to the heat of the moment, or something more. And if there was anything similar in her relationship with Alex. She toyed with the idea of calling her tomorrow to see.

CHAPTER THIRTY

Dusty was in a mental fog as she drove the thirty miles from her home in Carnation into the city to meet with Teggy. She had been able to avoid her since she had been back, but she had to meet with her today to talk about her next project. She hoped Teggy would be so excited about the book's outline, emailed to her moments before Dusty set out for Seattle, that she'd forget to grill her about how things were going with her.

She'd done a pretty good job so far of hiding that anything was wrong, she thought. She had been pretty quiet when Teggy picked her up at the airport, but she had passed that off as exhaustion from her flight and the ordeal on the mountain. She didn't mention what she had found out at the lodge. It turned out that her cabin was one of the ones that had sustained major damage. A large cedar had crashed through its huge picture window. Had she not been hiking with Morgan when the earthquake hit, she could have been severely injured—or worse.

She couldn't help but think of all the times that Morgan had saved her. She saved her from her near panic attack at the club when they first met, saved her from getting crushed in her cabin at the workshop, saved her when she froze up on the mountain and almost got buried by the landslide. The list went on and on. All Dusty had done in return was hurt her. She couldn't risk doing that to her again. Wouldn't. Morgan would be better off with her out of her life. She was sure of it.

When she reached the South Lake Union neighborhood, Dusty parked her car and made her way to Teggy's office, mentally reviewing what she wanted to say. And not say. She wasn't sure how long she would be able to talk to Teggy and not bring Professor Morgan West into the conversation. Teggy had a way of pulling things out of her.

"About your outline," said Teggy, wasting no time.

"Well, hello to you too. Let me get settled, thank you very much." Dusty poured a hearty amount of sugar into her coffee and made her way to the comfy leather chair that she favored when in Teggy's office.

"Are you sure you want to go through with this?"

"Yes, I am sure that I want to write about this. I think it will help others, don't you?"

"Oh, absolutely. Especially now that you have *Reservations* under your belt, you could give voice to a lot of kids."

"I know that. That's why I want to write about it."

"Why now?"

"Why now, what?"

"Why now do you all of a sudden want to write about what you experienced? About being homeless?"

"I don't know. I just think it's time," said Dusty, her thoughts drawn back to when she shared her story with Morgan. She could almost feel Morgan's arms around her when she embraced her afterward...

Her daydreaming was interrupted by Teggy.

"Well, I am one hundred percent behind you on this. And I am proud of you too. Writing about ending up homeless because you are gay will help a lot of kids and shed some much needed light on the topic," said Teggy. "Can you get me a draft by December?"

When Dusty didn't respond, she tried again.

"Well, can you?"

"Can I what?" Dusty had been reliving the night she and Morgan kissed after she had fallen.

"Get me a draft by December?"

"What? Yeah, I should be able to do that," said Dusty, fiddling with one of the large metal rivets ornamenting her chair and thinking about Morgan.

"Dusty. Earth to Dusty."

"Yes, yes, I can get you a draft by next year."

"I said December."

"I'm pretty sure you said next year."

"I said no such…" She'd avoided Teggy's gaze, but her agent didn't have to look her in the eyes to know something was wrong. "What is it?"

"What is what?"

"What is bothering you? You have avoided me long enough. I mean, I knew something was up when I picked you up at the airport."

"No, you didn't," Dusty said, finally making eye contact.

"I did. Now come on. It's time to spill the beans."

"Oh, God. I hate that expression. Can't you say something more along the lines of 'Let's hear it'? Or 'Out with it' or…"

"You're stalling, and you're not being funny."

"I am doing no such thing, and I am being funny. Christ, can't we just talk about the project, for crying out loud?"

"No, we can't. You aren't yourself. What happened, Dusty? When are you going to tell me about what happened in Idaho?"

"What on earth are you talking about?" Dusty said, taking too big a gulp of her hot coffee. "Shit," she said, closing her eyes at the pain. "See what you're doing to me?"

"Don't blame drinking hot coffee too fast on me, young lady. Out with it."

"Really, there is nothing to tell. I was almost buried by a landslide, survived, ate crap army food for three days." *Fell in love*, Dusty thought. "And now I'm home. Seriously, that is all that happened. I'm just tired, that's all."

"You are so full of shit. I'm not touching your project until you talk to me." Teggy folded her arms.

"You wouldn't do that."

"Oh, yes, I would, Dusty. I need you to be clearheaded if you are going to write about this. It will take a lot out of you—not to mention you are going to have to be careful how you write this one."

"I know that. I'm thinking of crafting it as an allegory."

"Oh." Her eyes lit up. "Very interesting... Have you thought of...? No." Teggy moved out from behind her desk to stand in front of Dusty. "First things first. Spill it, spill the beans. You're most definitely going to need to be one hundred percent for something like this and right now you are more like forty percent, maybe fifty."

"Jesus." Still...if Dusty had learned anything from Morgan it was that talking about things that were bothering her could make her feel a whole lot better. She found the courage to meet Teggy's eyes and took a deep breath. "I fell in love with her."

"What? With who? When?"

"With her, with Morgan."

"Whoa whoa whoa. Wait, you fell in love with Morgan—Professor West?" Teggy shook her head. "You were up there for all of three days. How is that even possible?"

"The night that I got into Idaho..."

"The night you got to Idaho, you met Morgan?"

"Yeah. But—well, sort of. The night I got into Idaho, I went to a club in Boise. I was going to get together with the flight attendant that I met on my flight." She looked at Teggy. Would Teggy judge her? But no, she wouldn't. She never had.

"Go on," said Teggy.

"Well, the flight attendant didn't show. I was about to leave the club when Morgan—"

"Morgan was at the club?"

"Yeah, she was at the club, but I didn't know it was Morgan. She and I didn't exactly exchange names. Well, I told her my name—"

"Wait a minute. She didn't get that maybe the new face at the club named Destiny was her guest speaker?"

"I said my name was Dusty."

"I see."

"She knew my name, but I didn't know it was her. Besides, even if I had learned her name, I was expecting someone older. You said she was your old—"

"Yes, my 'old friend.'" She laughed, and Dusty shot her a look. "Sorry, go on."

"Well, even if I had learned her name, I doubt I would have put the two together."

"Okay, so you left with a blonde who just happened to be Morgan?" Dusty shot Teggy another sharp look. "Sorry."

"Yeah, I left with a blonde who just happened to be Morgan. I forgot my coat and *she—she* practically chased me down to give it to me, and well—" Dusty told Teggy the story of the rest of that night. The PG-13 version.

"Jesus, so you slept with a blond stranger who turned out to be Professor West? What are the odds?"

"Yeah, I know. Sometimes I hate small towns. Trust me, it was supposed to be a one-time thing. I tried to avoid her at the workshop, but—"

"Jesus, of course you did. I told you to be nice. She's a friend of mine."

"I know. I was nice. I tried to avoid her and she totally called me out on it. She called me an ass, for crying out loud." Dusty smiled. "Well, that is why I was up hiking with her, because I was trying to be nice. Trying to be normal instead of..." She looked back down at rivet on the chair. "Instead of how I usually act with women I run into after... You know. After."

"I know, Dusty. It's okay. So you were trying to be nice—normal—and you went hiking with her. That *was* nice. But still, you were up there with her in her uncle's cabin for all of three days and you fell in love with her?"

Dusty nodded. "I'm not sure how it happened either. I simply started loving her. Actually, that's not true. I think I loved her from the moment I laid eyes on her."

Dusty thought of all the things that she had told Morgan and how good it made her feel to share those things about herself. It was like her heartache had been blown away from her, layer by layer, until she had revealed herself like a polished stone. Morgan had seen her before and after and everything in between.

"She is the reason why I feel like I can write this next book project. She helped me be able to talk about it and made me realize that I can help others by sharing what happened to me. And I love her for that. I need her for that." She felt tears well up in her eyes.

"Dusty, that is so beautiful. Why are you so sad? Doesn't Morgan feel the same way?"

"I don't know," said Dusty. She knew that Morgan liked her, liked having her body, but she didn't know if Morgan loved her. She was too scared to find out. She didn't want to take herself to a place where she could get hurt.

"What do you mean you don't know? Haven't you been talking to her?" Teggy said.

"No. Because that is not all that happened."

"Go on."

"I hurt her."

"What do you mean? Like physically?"

Dusty nodded her head in agreement. "Yeah, I did. Well, not by my hand, but it might as well have been me pushing her down the side of the bank."

"What happened?" asked Teggy, obviously baffled at what she was hearing.

Dusty told her that part of the story. Teggy stared at her.

"That was not your fault."

"It was! It was my fault. If I hadn't run out, she never would have—"

"Stop. You can't think like that. She made her own decision and went out to look for you. It was an accident. That could have happened to you. It wasn't your fault."

Dusty was silent for a moment as she tried to gather her thoughts. "It *feels* like it was my fault and if that—if her getting hurt—is any indication of what it would be like to be with someone like me, then she would be better off without me," she said, tears welling up in her eyes again. "But I love her and she is all I think about."

"Oh, Dusty," Teggy sighed. "That is not how it works, kid. You have to go back to Idaho and tell her how you feel. Just knowing will help you tremendously with this next book project."

"I know, but I can't," she whispered.

"Why?"

"I don't know. I don't think it's a good idea. Maybe I should just email her. You have her email, right?"

"Yes, but..." Teggy took Dusty's chin in her hand, tilting her face so she could look her in the eyes. "Hey, Dusty, it will be okay. But you need to go there—look her in the eyes—if you really want to know how she feels. You have to put yourself out there sometimes in life. Just like you did with *Reservations*. And look at all the positive and good things that have happened to you and to those around you as a result."

"You're right. But I don't think I can handle knowing how she really feels."

"You need to at least find out." Then Teggy blurted, "Oh God, I didn't think anything of it until now, but about a month ago, she sent me an email asking about you, wanting to know if you were okay. All I said was that you were surviving, doing well."

"Wait, what? She did?"

"Yeah, she did. You need to visit her and talk to her. She deserves that and so do you. If you love her, there must have been something you felt with her, a connection of some sort."

"I don't think I can handle it if she rejects me. I can't."

"But you have to try, Dusty. Go back there, try. Fight for her. What do you think she is feeling right about now? Have you emailed her even once or called her to let her know that you are settled and getting along? You know, asked her how she is doing, how her ankle is?"

"No," Dusty said. It hit her then how upset Morgan might be feeling. She knew Morgan had wanted more from her, especially after that night that they had kissed and she had held her until they had fallen asleep. "I don't have her number or email or—"

"You know that I have all of her info, Dusty. Besides, you know how to Google things."

"I know. I'm a coward."

"No, you're not. I get it—it is scary, it's Idaho, and there are a lot of what-ifs to think about."

"Yeah, like what if I get there and tell her how I feel and she doesn't feel the same way or has another lover?"

"I highly doubt she will have another lover." Teggy laughed.

"Or what if she *does* feel the same way? She lives there, I live here. It's impossible for anything—"

"Oh, you will figure it out," said Teggy, patting Dusty's hand reassuringly. "You're a smart girl, but first find out what she feels for you. You will feel a lot better and can devote one hundred percent of yourself to your next book project. Besides, I am sick of your moping around." She embraced Dusty. "And you are coming over this weekend for dinner, okay?"

"Okay, I will." She relented. "Thanks, Tegs."

"Don't start with the 'Tegs,' Destiny."

Dusty laughed, thinking back to the times Morgan had called her Destiny when she was pissed at her. The memories made her feel warm inside.

CHAPTER THIRTY-ONE

During the drive back to her farmhouse, Dusty wondered if she really would go through with it—with going back to Boise to see Morgan.

When she had gotten to the lodge that morning, she had thought about waiting for her. She would need help getting out of the lodge, with her ankle as bad as it was. That was before she overheard Morgan's sister talking about having come there to take her back to Boise. That all but settled it—it would be better if she just left. No need to get in the way. It seemed to her, actually, that the fact that she was no longer needed was a sign that she should not take this thing with Morgan any further, that she should get out of town and let Morgan be. She had faced Idaho and survived it—literally—and it was time to move the hell on.

Every thought she had was of Morgan, however. She went home, then left almost immediately for another round of *Reservations* promotions—this time in the Southwest—hoping the work would help distract her sufficiently. It didn't. Trying to slip back into her old routines, she had brought a woman from the bar back to her hotel in Santa Fe, but she ended up kicking her out before anything happened.

Her hands tightened on the steering wheel. It was Morgan she wanted, damn it. She was tired of masking her feelings. She had tried to get her out of her system, but Morgan was lodged deep in her heart. She didn't get anything from other women, feeling only emptiness when she was with them.

Since coming home from New Mexico a month ago, she had tried to keep herself busy with projects around her farm. She had done a lot of writing. She replaced the roof on her barn. It was too late to plant anything in the greenhouse, but she did anyway. She took her horses on a little weekend campout and even watched several sunrises.

Her thoughts kept taking her back to the cabin and to Morgan and what it had felt like to connect with her. It was out on the trail that it hit her—what her parents had done to her when they kicked her out of their house. Not only had they taken away her ability to trust others, they had taken away her ability to love. She wondered how much love, how many friendships she had missed out on by pushing people away from her. She wasn't going to let her parents or her past continue to hurt or control her anymore, she decided. She knew what she had to do.

CHAPTER THIRTY-TWO

"I can't believe you were stranded up there for three days! Whatever did you do?" said Alex as she worked on her dinner of heirloom tomato gazpacho with avocado sorbet.

It was mid-July and it was hot. Morgan was glad that she had followed through with connecting with Alex if only for the much-needed distraction from the intense summer session. The condensed academic schedule felt longer to her than those of past summers, and she knew why.

Morgan and Alex had met up at the Bardenay restaurant in the Basque part of Boise. The food was good, but it was the gin, distilled there, that made it worth standing in line for a table. Morgan had never been shy about revealing cleavage, something the silky, lightweight V-neck tank top she was wearing achieved quite handily, but the glances Alex was taking at her breasts weren't stirring her like they did when she caught Dusty looking at her that way.

"The first day—believe it or not—I slept. I was so exhausted from everything from school, from trying to keep us from getting buried from the landslide. Poor Destiny"—Morgan referred to Dusty as Destiny whenever possible, knowing that Dusty was a private person—"was probably bored to death while I slept the first day away."

"Oh yeah, I forgot you were up there with Destiny del Carmen. What was that like? What is she like? What does she even look like?"

Morgan took a moment to compose herself before she continued, thinking about how Dusty looked.

"Oh, she's absolutely beautiful. Kind of serious in her own way. Her eyes are dark. And her hair...her skin is so...she is so..."

Her blathering was cut short by the perplexed look on Alex's face. "She's nice," Morgan said. "She was great. I mean, we just talked a lot and passed the time away drinking wine and whiskey and sitting around the fire. There wasn't much we could do in between the storms."

She was thinking about Dusty returning to the cabin soaked from getting their firewood that one day and how her wet shirt had clung to her body. She bit her lower lip, becoming aroused at the thought of how Dusty's breasts had felt against her when she had held her tight the night she had fallen.

Morgan hoped Alex couldn't see her real feelings in her eyes. She didn't think she could—the two of them had never really connected emotionally.

"How did you hurt your ankle again?" Alex said.

"I twisted it in the landslide that almost buried us alive. But, then, I hurt it worse when I fell down the side of the trail."

"Wait, what? You fell down the side of a trail?"

"Yeah, stupid, I know. But I was out looking for...I was careless. The ground was so muddy and I wasn't careful and slipped off the side of the trail, down the bank. God, it was horrible—embarrassing too."

"You poor thing. I can rub your feet tonight if you want," Alex said with that look in her eye, placing her hand over Morgan's. The look, the touch—neither of them did anything for her anymore. "I bet you had to rely pretty heavily on Destiny?"

"Yeah, I did." Morgan took her hand away. "Poor thing had to do practically everything for us. She was great. She helped tremendously, especially the night I got hurt. She..." *Held me, said things to me, made me feel safe—and then she left...* "She was great. I miss her, believe it or not."

"How is she doing? Do you keep in touch?"

"No, and I don't know. I haven't heard from her since."

"Well, I am glad you are home and all that is behind you. I missed you and we were all worried when you were up there and no one knew anything," Alex said. "Do you want to come over tonight? You haven't been over in such a long time." She reached over again to Morgan, stroking her hand with her fingers.

"No, I shouldn't. I've got to be up early tomorrow. Got essays to grade, darn summer quarter midterms... It's intense right now and all. Besides—"

"Please, since when has grading essays kept you from coming over? What is really bothering you?"

"Nothing. I really do have a lot of grading to do and some funders are coming tomorrow to assess one of my programs."

Alex looked down. She wasn't dumb. "It's her, isn't it? Destiny? You lit up when you talked about her tonight. And you've practically flinched every time I have touched you."

"I'm sorry," whispered Morgan. "I'm sorry."

"Sorry? What are you talking about? I thought you wanted to spend time with me. Why did you invite me out if you didn't want to..."

Morgan's eyes welled up with tears. "I'm...trying to move on, I guess. I thought that if I was with you, if you and I could pick up where we left off before"—*Dusty*—"before the workshop, then maybe I would forget about her. I didn't mean to lead you on."

"I see." Alex looked intently into Morgan's soft brown eyes and then down to her lips. She reached under the table to caress Morgan's knee, making her way up her leg to just beneath the hem of the shorts she was wearing. "Come home with me and let's see if I can't take your mind off her. Give me—give us—another chance."

"Okay," said Morgan, her breath ragged, even though the whole time Alex was touching her she was thinking about Dusty. "Okay."

The two left their meals unfinished, though Morgan downed her gin and Alex's too. They paid their bill and walked to Alex's apartment nearby. Morgan didn't know how she was going to get through being with Alex, but it was too late to turn back now.

CHAPTER THIRTY-THREE

As Dusty approached South Montana Road, the smell of farmland filled her nostrils, overwhelming her senses. The odors of mint and alfalfa were heavy in the air around her, and while they smelled clean and pure and sweet, the memories they evoked were sour ones.

The steering wheel of the car was sticky and hot under her grip. She was holding it, she realized, as if letting go would mean certain death. She loosened her grip and took a deep breath, calming herself as she approached the high school she had been kicked out of years ago. If she couldn't do even this, there wasn't much point in going forward with the proposed book. She gritted her teeth and drove resolutely down memory lane.

She recognized the changes instantly. The old letter board marquee, the one that had held Bible verses and notices and welcomed passersby, had been replaced by an electronic version, new, modern and high-tech. Its current message:

SCHOOL STARTS MONDAY, AUGUST 25
WE ARE ACCEPTING NEW STUDENTS
JOURNEY TO EXCELLENCE THROUGH HIM

The big white house that the asshole P.E. teacher had lived in was gone and in its place was an open field of brown grass. Massive syringa and elm surrounded the school grounds still, rooted firmly place, oblivious to the comings and goings of the years and the students with them.

As Dusty pulled onto the school property she noticed the senior class gift from what would have been her class had she completed high school there. It was a large decorative rock which read: GEM STATE JAGUARS, CLASS OF 1999. The image of the school mascot, the Jaguar, with his game face on, took up most of the surface of the rock.

She pulled into a space in the lot and parked. She had done it, she was on school property. "Damn," she said, realizing that she was not alone, even though it was Sunday, a day when usually nothing would be going on. "Now what?" she whispered, looking at the handful of cars parked around her.

Mustering up her courage, she got out of her car and approached the main building, a large red brick structure surrounded by evergreens. She didn't expect the doors to be open, but they were. She was greeted as soon as she walked in.

"Can I help you?" said an older woman, her tone gentle and inviting.

"No. I mean, yes," Dusty stammered.

"Do you have a student you would like to admit?" the woman said eagerly.

"No. Nothing like that. I used to go to school here. It was a long time ago. I was in the area and…"

"I see, and you wanted to take a trip down memory lane?"

"Yes, exactly." She smiled nervously.

"What year did you graduate?" said the woman as she turned, walking into the building.

"I didn't. At least not from here." She decided to keep the details of her sordid past to herself. "I kind of wanted to look around, I guess. But if you are busy, it's okay. I am probably trespassing." Dusty turned to make her way out of the door. "Thanks, though."

"No, wait, it's no trouble. Come on back. I could use a break to tell you the truth. I am working on the budget at the moment, so good timing on your part. Things have changed quite a bit, haven't they?"

"Yes, they have. I like the new electronic billboard."

"Yes, we got that recently, thanks to an anonymous donor. We finally got new, much-needed windows on all the buildings too." She seemed to notice Dusty's hesitation. "Would you like to have a look around? I'll show you all the changes. School starts in a couple of weeks so there are a few student workers around, some maintenance people and an eager teacher or two. I'm Mrs. Davis, uh, Karen. What did you say your name was?"

"Oh, sorry, I'm Dusty." She extended her hand, and Mrs. Davis shook it.

"How long ago did you attend school here, if I can ask?"

"I was supposed to graduate in 1999. I left halfway through my senior year."

"Heavens, I bet that was tough on you. Did your family relocate or something?"

"Yes, we did." Dusty felt confident in her response. She started to feel more at ease.

"Do you keep in touch with any of your old classmates?"

"Not really." *As in not at all*, she thought as she followed Mrs. Davis. They exited the main administration building and headed for the boys' dorm first, then the girls' dorm, passing a handful of students working on the school farm. They toured the school's newly renovated cafeteria, exited the café and approached the music building.

"Did you play an instrument or sing in the choir by chance?" asked Mrs. Davis as they entered the building and the band room. Dusty was too caught up in memories to reply.

* * *

"Let's cut class." Andrea had a mischievous look in her eyes as she went to the gym's double doors. They led to an alley used for the school's odd-sized deliveries. It also served as a hidden route to the music hall and private music instruction rooms. Not many people knew about the shortcut passage—mostly school administrators and some student workers—but Destiny and Andrea did. Quite well, in fact.

"We're going to get caught one of these days!" Destiny said as she made sure the coast was clear for their departure from weights class. They were supposed to be working on their own time. The P.E. teacher split his time between basketball practice and keeping an eye on the weights-class students, who were mostly there to get an easy credit. So sneaking out was simple enough.

"So what, fuck them," Andrea said. "We're nearly graduated. We can do what we want whenever we want, isn't that right?"

"That's right." Destiny said as she grabbed Andrea around the waist and pulled the golden blonde into herself. "And I will do whatever I want to you whenever you want." She reached under her shirt to feel her breasts with one hand and caressed her between her legs with the other. She placed soft kisses on Andrea's neck and felt the girl slowly wilt in her arms. The girl turned to kiss Destiny softly on the lips, looked into her eyes and smiled. They had started having sex the summer before and now took advantage of every opportunity they were alone, which wasn't much, to make love. In fact, they had even taken up hiking and fishing on the weekend, outdoor activities that gave them an excuse to be alone together, outside, where walls and barriers were removed.

Messing around in the music building was their latest secret escape. They knew it was risky, but they didn't care. Two girls kissing or even holding hands wasn't exactly an acceptable form of interaction at their religious high school. But today they couldn't wait for the school day to end.

They made their way into the music building, where they heard the sound of one of their classmates finishing up her private flute class with an instructor.

"Oh my God, why aren't they done yet?" whispered Andrea. "All her damn lessons and she's not even that good."

"Yeah, she should be out by now." Destiny looked at her watch. Well aware of when Kelly's private music tutoring ended, they had started taking the opportunity to occupy the empty room as soon as she and her instructor had left. That gave them a good half hour to mess around. Upon seeing the light to the room darken and hearing the voices recede out of the building, they moved into the dark, cool room. Both were eager to finish what they had started in the passageway.

"Finally." Destiny pulled the willing girl into her, holding her tightly against herself. "All mine."

"I can't wait. Dest, hurry, you got to touch me," Andrea whimpered into her lips.

As commanded, Destiny undid the button of her partner's jeans and reached inside to feel her burning desire. "Wow. You're wet," she whispered into Andrea's neck. She pulled her shirt up and her bra down and took Andrea's breasts into her mouth, at the same moment entering her below. "I wish I could taste you now. I can't wait until we're at college and we can do this whenever we want," she said as she worked Andrea into a frenzy, supporting her partner's wild responses and movements. She nearly had her at the edge.

"In the meantime," panted Andrea, "we're just going to have to…make do… I love you, Dest," she said in Destiny's ear. She let herself go completely, muffling a scream of pleasure against her shoulder.

"I love…" Destiny's declaration was cut short as the door opened and there stood Kelly.

* * *

"Well, did you?" asked Mrs. Davis.

"Huh? said Dusty, broken out of her flashback. "Oh, no, I didn't really have an ear for music." She chuckled, remembering the *music* she and her high school girlfriend had made in the band room when they skipped classes.

After touring the music building, the two made their way back to the red brick building which housed the administration, the classrooms, the library, the gym and the school chapel and made their way up the stairs to where most of the classes were taught. On the walls at the top were large framed photos of each of the graduating classes, starting with the Class of 1918. They made their way down one long hallway and up the other. Finally, there it was, the photo of her classmates from the Class of 1999.

"Here is your class," said Mrs. Davis.

"Yes, there they are." Dusty examined the faces of people in the small graduating class. Her friends. Her enemies: Christy and Kelly. And Andrea. She looked beautiful, her long hair a golden cascade down her shoulders. She must have managed to convince everyone that their little interaction had simply been a game. She looked as if she hadn't a care in the world. Her smile was a frozen moment, a time and a place where all was new and exciting and promising. Catching her own reflection in the glare of the glass, Dusty gave herself a rueful smile and saucy wink, stopping her mind from taking her to that dark place she had worked so hard to get out of.

"Did you know anyone in the class?" Dusty asked.

"Not really, I was hired a handful of years ago. My husband and I are not from the area. We moved here from Oregon. We have two kids about to graduate from school here," Mrs. Davis said proudly. "My husband teaches computer science and I am one of the school's administrators." She noted Dusty's fading interest. "But I can tell you who would." She motioned down the hall to an open classroom. "Mr. Whalen."

"Wow, he still teaches here?" said Dusty, amazed and anxious.

"He sure does. He keeps up with a lot of our students and our alumni. He is still very much involved in youth activities even though his own kids have long since grown up." Dusty followed her to the classroom.

Mrs. Davis knocked gently. "Mr. Whalen, how are things going? Are we interrupting?"

"Absolutely not, come on in," he said as he got up out of his chair, slowly. The man was obviously past the age of retirement, but he still had the look of a first-year teacher.

"This is Dusty, she used to go to school here…"

"Dusty?"

"Destiny del Carmen." Dusty noted his confusion and then the nod of his head as the light turned on.

"Oh my goodness," he said. "Yes, I remember you quite well. The name Dusty threw me for a loop there. I thought I was losing my name-to-face recognition skills." He laughed. "What a blast from the past and you're all grown up and a writer now!" He grabbed Dusty's hand and her entire body shook from his bearlike grip. Dusty couldn't help but smile at his warm and welcoming personality. She was surprised that he knew she was a writer and amazed when he went to retrieve one of several copies of *Reservations* from his bookshelf.

"We're going to be studying this work of art this coming semester," he said. "Wow, welcome home, kid!" He thumped the book into the palm of his hand, his eyes wide.

"Gosh, you didn't tell me you were a writer." Mrs. Davis beamed. "I remember ordering those books for his class. What an inspiring read, what a story." They stared at Dusty in awe. The chimes of a phone brought everyone to attention.

"Aww. I hate to leave, but I have a family coming in soon who is interested in sending two daughters here. Dusty, if you would let me know when you leave, I would appreciate it." Mrs. Davis walked out the door. "Have fun getting reacquainted. I'll see you on your way out, Dusty."

"Of course, and thank you for the trip down memory lane."

"Come sit down," Mr. Whalen said. "How have you been? Do you live here now?" He said, bombarding her with questions. "Gosh, I haven't seen you since…" His smile faded. "Oh yes, you were…"

"Yes, I was suspended from here for…"

"I remember." He saved her from having to give voice to what had happened. "You were basically outed to your parents in the worst possible way, weren't you?"

"Pretty much." Her eyes dropped to the floor. The memory was clear and crisp in her mind. Not so much the heartache. She finally felt that she was moving beyond all of that. Thanks to Morgan. The thought of her made her smile; she knew that she would be okay no matter what happened. Morgan had changed that part of her forever.

"How are your parents now?" Mr. Whalen said. "Gosh, your whole family kind of fell off the face of the earth after you were suspended. Last we heard your folks sent you to Auburn to finish out your senior year and y'all had relocated to…Oregon, was it?"

"Oregon?" she whispered. "To be honest, I haven't been in contact with them in a very long time," she said, her voice fading. Mr. Whalen didn't know and she suspected that none of her parents' friends and acquaintances knew that they had kicked her out and disowned her. Who knew what story they came up with.

"I see, and what brings you back to the school?" He motioned for her to sit and pulled out a couple of chairs.

"I am doing some research on a new book project."

"Wow, is that right? Does it take place here at our school?" He seemed eager to listen. His smile faded and his reactions were more serious as he listened to her story.

She filled him in on her next project and the angle she was taking with it. Told him about what had actually happened with her family. About being alone and homeless in Washington. She didn't know why she decided to tell her former teacher her life story, but she was glad that she did. His reaction gave her a sense of validation, made her feel that what she had experienced was unjust and unfair and that she could write the story and people would believe her. She could help others who had faced similar exile from their families. She felt even more empowered to tackle the project than before she had arrived at the school.

"Wow," Mr. Whalen said. "You will help a lot of kids and it will resonate with parents too, as I am sure you know. It was such a shame that the two of you were suspended for being yourselves. It is too bad that the school didn't have a group or any outlet for you kids at the time. There isn't really anything like that now either, but the students are much more open now than they were back when you were in school. Do you still keep in touch with Andrea?"

"I haven't spoken to her since the day we got caught."

* * *

"Oh wow! Oh my God. I like, left my music book behind," Kelly said. Her friend Christy was next to her. They were staring at Andrea and Destiny in disgust.

"Well, get your book and get the fuck out!" Destiny said.

"Destiny! Jesus," said Andrea. "Hey, Kelly, we're just messing around. It's nothing serious, it's like a dare, so…"

"A dare, that is disgusting! Oh my God!" Kelly and Christy left as quickly as they arrived.

"Fucking shit." The girls said it in tandem as they pulled themselves together, still breathing heavily, frozen with fear at being exposed. Kelly and Christy were the most notorious gossips in their class.

"A dare? Why did you say it was a dare?" Destiny said.

"I don't know. What was I supposed to say?" Andrea tidied herself up, her cheeks pink and her hair in disarray. "I was as caught off guard as you were. Shit! Sorry, I didn't know what to say."

"Okay. Well, we got to think! Go, go and get them, go talk to them. Tell them whatever. Seriously, this can't get out, not now. My parents will kill me," Destiny pleaded. Andrea was better at convincing people to do things they didn't want to do.

"Okay, okay. I'll see what I can do. Whatever happens, Dest, I love you, and this changes nothing, okay? Whatever happens, we're still together, okay, no matter what, I'll still be with you." She kissed Destiny's palm.

"I know and I love you too, and hey, fuck them, right?" She took one final kiss from her lover. "Go on. I'll meet you back in weight class, okay?"

"Okay, see you in class."

* * *

"Destiny, I am sorry no one reached out to you to make sure you were okay," Mr. Whalen said. "I guess we, I mean, speaking for myself, I thought that your family moved. We have kids that get expelled or transfer out of our school every now and again and when people leave, we don't usually hear from them again."

"Thank you for that," Dusty said, genuinely meaning it. "I've been an angry person for a good part of my life, but I am trying to move on. I am hoping this project can help with that."

"Oh, I am positive it will." He looked at Dusty, studying her. "Are you wondering about Andrea?"

"A little," she said. "To be honest, I haven't thought about her in a very long time. Is she still in the area?"

"Well, yes and no. She had moved back to be with her folks, but has since left. The only reason I know anything about her is because her dad is on the school board here, heavily involved and a major donor." He added, "He had hoped she would stay, had been trying to get Andrea to join the board or teach or do something here at the school." He reminisced. "Well, she is Andrea Adams now. Divorced actually, twice divorced."

"Twice?"

"That's right. This last time it ended badly, according to her father. Her husband was abusive, he had a bad temper...they both had anger issues, from what I hear. She had been living in Manhattan, working as a high-powered attorney. She did really well from what I've heard, doesn't have to work anymore if she doesn't want to."

"Oh, well, that's good. But horrible—the way it ended. I didn't really know that she had a temper though."

"Yes, when I spoke with her father, I was surprised to hear about that part too. She wasn't like that in high school. People change and high school was a long time ago. Maybe it was her high-pressure job."

"Perhaps," she said, thinking that something else was probably triggering Andrea's anger.

"After divorcing her second husband she sold her practice and moved back to be with her parents. A year later her mom passed away. Sad story. Cancer, the aggressive kind," Mr. Whalen said with a sigh. "The two of them, her and her father, were heartbroken."

"I can imagine." She genuinely meant it. She had known Andrea's parents well, having been best friends—*lovers*—with their daughter and a friend of the family since elementary school. She knew what it was like to lose a family member.

"An attorney, huh?" She chuckled, remembering how Andrea had balked at the idea of following in her parents' footsteps. The idea that she actually became a lawyer didn't shock her either. Andrea could shift between emotions and personalities on a whim. She would talk behind a teacher's back and be their best student to their face. Or turn on the tears when she thought she was going to get in trouble with her parents, only to laugh at their stupidity in the next moment. "Lawyers!" she would say. And her ultimate act: from making love with Destiny in the band room to being a complete stranger to her less than an hour after they were caught, acting as if nothing had ever happened between them. Erasing years of friendship and love that they had built together. Letting her fall off the face of the earth.

"I bet she is a really great lawyer," she said.

"Well, in her defense, she's not entirely on the dark side." Mr. Whalen laughed. "Her father says that she now works with the Innocence Project, so I know she still has a heart." Dusty laughed with him.

"Well, that is good. At least there is hope." She smiled.

"She lives in Portland now, but comes back and forth quite a bit. I am sure you can see her if you want. Her dad still lives at the same house she grew up in, believe it or not."

At that, Dusty took a deep breath and stood. "I should go. Thank you for…everything. It means a lot."

"The pleasure is all mine, seriously. Before you go, would you?" He eyed his copies of *Reservations*.

"Of course."

Dusty autographed all the copies of *Reservations* for his incoming students. She wrote a lengthy note in his and said that she would maybe, possibly, consider, at some point being a guest speaker for him in the future. Instead of a handshake, she received a hearty hug.

"Good luck to you and your project, Dusty."

"Thank you," she said, making her way down the long hallway, stopping only long enough to tell Mrs. Davis that she was leaving.

* * *

Dusty left the campus feeling a little more at ease and a lot more empowered to tackle her book project. And to reconnect with Morgan, no matter the outcome. With each step she took, it was if she was emerging from a turbulent ocean. Old feelings stilled, feelings that she was so used to, that had come and gone as reliably as the swells of the waves pulling at her to retreat back into its depths. She no longer felt the familiar blind anger she'd always experienced when she thought about her parents living their life as if they didn't have a daughter. Though that wall would need to come down...soon. She had questions and she wanted answers. She wanted to understand them better, she needed to understand their mindset. She vowed she would make an effort to reconnect with them, for her own sake.

She no longer felt sad when she thought about Andrea or about Christy and Kelly and her old high school. What her old teacher had shared with her about Andrea had given her a new understanding of her first girlfriend. She had done what any seventeen-year-old would do when she was outed by her peers—put herself first.

No, Dusty didn't hate Andrea. She felt sorry for her. At least in Auburn she had had Robby, a positive influence, an entire family that supported her and who she was. Likely Andrea had had no one to see her through her confusion.

Only hope lived in Dusty's heart now. Hope for a positive future with the woman that had come into her life, turned it upside down, shown her how to move on and live in the moment. Who, most importantly, had taught her how to love again. She hoped to God that Morgan would let her back in, even though it had been more than three months since they had last spoken.

CHAPTER THIRTY-FOUR

"You what?"

"I went home with Alex last night. It was horrible! I used her. I called out Dusty's name when she was kissing me, and then I started crying. Jesus!" Morgan's face reddened and her hands moved to massage her head.

"Oh my God," said Rosalie. "You poor thing."

"Me, a poor thing? I feel awful for doing that to Alex, for using her like that."

"She will be all right. I mean, if Destiny was all you were talking about during your little date, then surely she had to know that you were in love with her. What was she thinking, asking you to go home with her? She should be the one that feels bad, not you—taking advantage of you like that." Rosalie had always known the best things to say to her to make her feel better. They had spent countless hours pouring their hearts out to each other about women and sex and life.

"I could've said no, but I was desperate. I mean, I fell in love with Dusty, hard, and I wanted to see if it was lust I was feeling," said Morgan, shaking her head. "But it wasn't. All this is so new to me, I've never really put so much focus on another person. But she, she pulled at me."

She had called up Rosalie early that morning intending to ask her to coffee and had lost it on the phone when she told her about Alex. Rosalie had to calm her down and kept her on the phone as she drove to Morgan's house. She spent the first hour holding her and listening to her.

"It's not your fault. Alex will be just fine," said Rosalie, still holding Morgan. The two were in her bed. The room was dark and the shades were drawn, despite the sunny day.

"I broke up with her. I broke it off—the on-and-off again. I can't anymore, not after what I felt with Dusty. I need something more," said Morgan, sniffling.

"Well, at least that chapter with Alex is over, right? It's all uphill from here, right?" said Rosalie. "Do you feel a little better?"

"A little," Morgan said.

CHAPTER THIRTY-FIVE

The night was young and women were flocking to the Balcony for the monthly ladies' night. Morgan was on the stool by the door, checking IDs. She would have rather been tending bar, but she didn't want to risk overextending herself and reinjuring her ankle. Everywhere she looked, she saw happy people. They were dancing, holding each other and having fun. Some were lost in their lover's embrace, kissing and loving each other.

But Morgan didn't let herself feel loneliness or sorrow. She was past that phase. She came to the conclusion that her time with Dusty was just that: a time she had spent with someone who had needed her in her life at that exact moment. She was glad she had met her and had been there to help her through her return to Idaho, which had been difficult but necessary to her healing process. Dusty had done what she had to do to protect herself, even if it was at Morgan's expense. She knew that now and was no longer angry. She would always wonder, though, what it would be like to have Dusty in her life full-time.

"You doing okay?" said Rosalie as she handed over a fresh iced tea, startling Morgan.

"Hey, thanks. Yeah, I'm fine."

"Yeah, the ladies are crazy tonight. It's hoppin' in here, huh?"

"Sure is," said Morgan. She pressed the cold glass to her forehead to cool herself down. "Hot too."

"No kidding. You need a break?"

"Nah, I'm good. I am enjoying myself. I haven't had to chase anybody down. It's been a good night so far."

She honestly meant it. She smiled at her friend. She had actually started to feel better in her heart. She was enjoying sitting in the entrance to the club, enjoying the soft breeze wafting through the hallway. It was nearing late August and sitting outside was nice, even at the eleven o'clock hour. "Hey, around last call, bring me a Long Island, will ya?"

"You got it, little sister. Hey, you still on for dinner tonight and a slumber party?"

"Yeah, that sounds fun."

The night progressed and the lines continued on. She took IDs and ran her black light over them, ensuring they weren't fake, looked each person up and down, stamped their wrists and let them in. She was in a rhythm, working through packs of people in their Saturday-night best, letting her thoughts drift, when someone handed her an ID from the state of Washington. She had seen a few out-of-state IDs throughout the night, but of course Washington always made her think of Dusty.

Her heart skipped a beat when she read the name on the card: Destiny del Carmen. Looking up in shock, she saw Dusty standing before her, looking utterly delicious. She was dressed in snug dark blue jeans and a bright white V-neck tank top with a howling wolf on it. The bright white was a contrast to her dark arms and her long wavy black hair, held high in a slicked-back ponytail.

Morgan had forgotten how Dusty looked in normal everyday clothes. All of the visions she had of Dusty were of her in Morgan's uncle's oversized clothes. Or naked.

She kept her emotions in check as she handed Dusty's ID back. "Your wrist," she said, holding out her hand for Dusty's. Her breath stuttered the moment she had it in her grasp. Trembling at the electric charge that coursed through her body when Dusty touched her, she took her wrist, stamped it and... her hands refused to release it. She wanted to hold on to it forever. She willed herself to let it go, and finally she did.

"Hi," said Dusty as she pulled her hand back, inspecting the invisible stamp that glowed only in the black light. "I thought I might find you here. Well, I was hoping I would." She smiled, but Morgan gave her nothing in response.

"How come you aren't tending bar?" she said, looking in that direction, unable, it seemed, to look Morgan in the eyes.

"My ankle still hurts, so sitting here is better for me than working behind the bar," Morgan said, trying to control her out-of-control heart.

"Oh." Dusty said awkwardly.

"So, are you going into the club or what?"

"No."

"Well, why are you here, Destiny?"

* * *

She smiled nervously. "There you go again, calling me Destiny. Guess I'm in trouble." She stuffed her hands in her pockets and ducked her head. "Of course I am. That's why I'm here. Can you leave? Can you come with me? I need to talk to you." She raised her head and searched Morgan's eyes for any hint of what they had had in the cabin in the mountains. She saw only hurt. Of course. What else should she expect?

"I can't," whispered Morgan.

"Oh, yeah. No, it's okay. I shouldn't have..." Dusty felt familiar pain wash over her.

"Shouldn't have what?" said Morgan. She motioned for Dusty to move out of the way so she could check the IDs of a group of girls and, smiling, summoned them forward. Dusty had thought night and day about that smile since leaving Idaho.

Seeing it again reinforced her sense that her decision to come to Boise had been worth it.

"I wanted to see if you were okay," she said as the group moved on. "Your foot, it seems better," she said. Again she got nothing in return. She was handling this all wrong. She felt her heart race and her eyes well up with tears. She blinked them away. "Did you need surgery or anything?"

"No, just PT. It's a lot better now." Morgan tucked a stray lock of hair behind her ear, closed her eyes and blinked back tears of her own.

"Oh, that's good. Okay, well, Morgan, you look…"

"Why didn't you say good-bye to me, Dusty?" Morgan reached out and touched Dusty's arm, her voice trembling as she trailed her finger down its length before pulling it back.

Dusty's eyes closed. "I want to explain that. Please let me. I'm sorry for making you feel like you didn't mean anything. So sorry. Please, can we go somewhere to talk?"

Morgan sighed heavily. "I can't leave now. But I get off at two. If you want to come back then…"

"Yes, of course I do. I'll come back. I promise."

* * *

As she prepared to process another group, Morgan watched Dusty retreat the way she had come. It took everything in her power to not follow her. She had looked into her eyes, hoping to see in them what she had seen in the cabin: desire, love, a future together. She had looked for it but hadn't seen a single trace. She wondered what Dusty was going to say. Whatever it was, she wasn't going to let her simply waltz back into her life. Not after all she had put her through.

Morgan took a deep breath and closed her eyes. When she opened them, she saw Rosalie approaching with her Long Island.

"Great fucking timing," she said as she grabbed the drink and took a hearty sip from the straw.

"Was that who I thought it was? That was Dusty, wasn't it?" said Rosalie. "She is breathtaking."

"I know. She really is, isn't she?" Morgan said. "Christ, she's coming back later. She wants to talk to me. I don't know if I can talk to her. Damn, I was honestly starting to get over her, to move on." She rubbed her hand against her forehead. "Shit, where should we go to talk? If I take her home, God knows what will happen. I can't do that to myself." She took another long sip.

"Hey, hey, slow down, honey. Breathe." Rosalie rubbed her friend's arm. "Give her a chance to say what she has to say, Morgan, and then go from there."

"She had three months—more than three months—to talk to me. She never emailed or called. Not once. I tried at least: I emailed her agent to ask about her. If she thinks she can just pop back into my life, she is going to be unpleasantly surprised when I tell her how it is."

Rosalie rubbed her friend's back. "Why don't you take her to my office? I'll be right down here waiting for you if you need me."

"No. No. It's too claustrophobic in there! I can hardly breathe out here."

"Morgan, slow down. Take some more deep breaths." She grabbed her friend's chin to lift her head up so she could look into her eyes. "I think you should let her explain. Tell her how you feel. Tell her that you fell in love with her, so she knows. From what I saw, she most definitely loves you too."

"Oh, please. How can you tell? I mean, how—"

"I could tell by the way she was looking at you. She had that look in her eyes."

"I can't, Rosalie," Morgan said, not caring now about the tears running down her cheeks. "I thought that I was over her. But Jesus—the sight of her—what she does to me…"

"You can and you will get through it."

"Shit, I hope so."

CHAPTER THIRTY-SIX

Last call came and went in agonizing slow-motion. Finally, at ten till two, Morgan made her way to Rosalie's tiny office to get her belongings. She stopped briefly to look down at the busy scene through the one-way glass. She saw people having fun. She saw lovers in embrace. They looked so happy.

Then she spotted Dusty. She had returned exactly at two o'clock like she said she would and was standing right outside the doors of the club. As people left, she couldn't help notice the number of women who looked at Dusty with desire. One of them actually took her hand and tried to drag her away.

She was stunning—so different from anyone that she had seen before in Boise. She was so utterly divine just being herself.

Realizing that she was keeping Dusty waiting, Morgan snapped out of her trance, grabbed her purse and headed down the stairs.

* * *

"Hi, Dusty," said Morgan. "So did you have another speaking engagement in Idaho and figured you would swing by for a good time?"

Dusty winced, hearing the anger in her voice. Anger that she deserved. "No, I came here to see you," she said. "Can we get out of here? Go somewhere private, where we can talk?"

"I really shouldn't, Dusty," Morgan said. "Where were you? I missed you. I was worried about you. You left again, didn't even say good-bye. Why do you keep doing that to me?"

"I'm sorry, Morgan. I don't know why I did that." Dusty shook her head. "But I do know that I missed you too. You were all I thought about." She reached out to Morgan, running her hand over her bicep. The heat she felt there instantly calmed her. It was as if she had been swimming too deep in the ocean and had finally reached the surface and air. "Can you please leave with me? I want to show you something. I need to talk to you."

"No." Morgan shook her head. "I'm sorry. You can't come and go as you please with people. I can't let you do that to me again. It's too painful. You of all people should know that." She shrugged Dusty's hand from her arm. "You made me feel really stupid for—for needing you so badly that last night. And to get down from the mountain and find you gone? And then not hear from you in three months? It felt…it really hurt, Dusty."

She drew herself up and looked Dusty in the eye. The words she said sounded rehearsed, like she'd been formulating them for months, but there was nothing artificial or dispassionate about them. "I can't and I won't let you do that to me again. I am sorry, but I have to protect myself and go on with my life. Please, you need to understand." She turned around to head back into the club to be with Rosalie.

Dusty couldn't believe what she had heard; she almost let herself fall down to her knees. She had tried to be positive on her trip to Boise, but in the back of her mind she had known that was likely to be Morgan's reaction. She knew too that she deserved it.

"I'm sorry, Morgan," Dusty whispered to herself. "So sorry." She straightened up. If she wanted Morgan in her life, she was going to have to fight for her, for her attention, for her love. She followed her into the club. "Please. Morgan," she said, desperation in her voice, tears running down her face. Everyone was looking at her except the one person she wanted to be looking.

"Morgan, do you want to know why I never asked you your name when we first met?" There was no response from the figure standing with her back to her. "Morgan, please," she begged. "Look at me. Do you want to know why?"

"Why?" Morgan said, turning to look at Dusty with tear-filled eyes of her own. The people left in the club fell silent.

"I didn't need to know your name. Your eyes were all I needed. I saw them and thought I could be lost in a foreign country and find you just by looking for them. And that—that realization—it scared the hell out of me. All I know how to do is run. I shouldn't have run from you, but I did and it was the worst decision I've ever made." She walked toward Morgan and took her hand in hers. "Please, will you come with me? Can I please talk to you?" She looked around at the many eyes on them. "Not here?"

Morgan closed her eyes and took a deep breath. "Dusty…" she whispered, clearly torn, then she looked over at Rosalie, who nodded her head, indicating that she understood.

"Where?"

"Come on. Follow me." Pulling gently on her hand, Dusty led her down the escalators to the street.

CHAPTER THIRTY-SEVEN

"If you think you are taking me to your hotel, you can think again."

"No, no hotel. Come on."

They approached a white Toyota Land Cruiser. Dusty pressed something on her key ring that started the engine and unlocked the doors.

"Is this yours?"

"Yeah."

"That is some rental," Morgan said.

"It's not quite a rental. Get in." Soon they were heading out of the city and eastbound on Interstate 84, bypassing all the places that Morgan thought Dusty could be taking her.

"Where are we going?" asked Morgan.

"To my place."

"To what?"

"The place where I am staying for a little bit. Sit tight, okay?" Dusty continued past the towns of Meridian and Nampa before finally taking one of the last Caldwell exits. Morgan stole

glances of Dusty—and caught Dusty doing the same of her—
but the two of them remained silent as the Toyota made its way
through the summer night.

About fifteen miles out of town they reached a dark driveway
and drove in. One by one, motion sensor lights clicked on,
illuminating a barbed-wire-lined gravel path. Dusty approached
a large ranch house nestled between tall syringa trees, pulled
into the driveway, parked next to a huge horse trailer and took
a deep breath.

"You're staying here?" said Morgan, her throat dry.

"For a little bit," she said as she turned the car off and got
out. "Come on."

Morgan let Dusty lead her to the front door, which opened
into the interior of a farm home that had been totally remodeled
inside. There was a large fireplace and a massive leather couch.
Picture windows took up nearly all the wall space, and built-in
dark-wood features gave the home a sophisticated feel. A few
moving boxes were stacked neatly against one wall, awaiting
someone's attention, but otherwise it was immaculate.

"I'm not quite unpacked yet, as you can see. The horses are
here and everything. What do you think?"

"What do I think about what?" Morgan said, perplexed.

"This," she said, looking around, "is where you're staying?"

"Yeah, well, I owe you another presentation to your students
and I don't welsh on my bets. Despite what you may think, I am
a woman of my word. Oh and this is for you," she said grabbing
a paper bag off the counter. "It's a bottle of Johnny Walker and
a hundred bucks." She held it out to Morgan, who only stared at
it. She placed it back on her counter. "Okay."

"You moved here to give a presentation to my students?"
Morgan said. "Why are you really here, Dusty? Come on, talk
to me."

"I'm going to try to write my next book from here." She
took a deep breath. "I am going to write about what happened
to me, what my parents did to me. Kicking me out because of
who I loved. I have thought a lot about what you said about
helping young homeless kids and I am going to do it."

"I'm going to donate all the proceeds to youth centers," she continued. "I need to be here to be able to write about it, here in Idaho. Where it happened to me, where I can research things myself and come to terms with everything. There are some things I need to make right too."

She smiled. "I've already gotten started on one. Guess what? I found Robby. Believe it or not he has been living in Washington State this whole time. He hasn't been sober in about fifteen years, but he remembers me." Her eyes grew teary. "He's not in good shape, not at all. I'm trying to figure out how I can help him."

"I'm so sorry. I know how much he means to you."

"I gave him a coloring book, like those adult ones, you know? And pencils to help him remember how much he loved drawing."

"That is a great start." Morgan shook her head. "But back up. Help me out here. I thought you hated being in Idaho. How will you ever write from here?"

"I do." Dusty shook her head. "I mean, I did hate it here, until…" She reached for Morgan's hand, leading her to the couch. "Until I met you. I met you, and my life was turned upside down, literally. I have thought of nothing but you since I left the mountain. I tried, Morgan, I tried to forget you, but I couldn't."

She rubbed her forehead. "I couldn't get you out of my thoughts, not for one waking moment. I realized that my parents, my mom and dad, the ones from Caldwell, they really hurt me when they left me in Washington. They sent me away to keep me from loving Andrea but in the process succeeded in keeping me from loving any other woman…until I met you. And I realized that it was time that I stop letting them hurt me."

She looked up at the tall ceiling. "You know, before you I thought I had it all figured out. The way to keep from being left was to leave first." She chuckled. "Absurd, right? My parents took from me the ability to love, to let myself be loved, to want to be loved. Christ, when I think of how many chances at love I missed out on, it makes me sad. But I am done with that chapter."

She stood up and turned toward Morgan. "I fell in love with you on that mountain, Morgan. Aside from hurting you badly all the times when I've run off, I think I've done fairly well. I think—I mean, I'm pretty positive—that I can take care of you. And if you want, that I can let you take care of me. That we could take care of each other like we did at the cabin. I'm not scared anymore. I won't run again. I have nowhere to run to anyway. I've found what I was looking for."

"What were you looking for, Dusty?" asked Morgan, her voice gentle.

"For you, Morgan, for your love. I am in love with you, all of you, every part of you. I'm going to have to dig deep to write this next book, and you—you give me the courage to do that and to be able to handle anything else that life throws at me. That's not why I came back here though. I'm okay to be in Idaho by myself now. You helped me figure that part out. I came back for *you*. I love you."

* * *

Dusty looked at her for a response, but Morgan didn't quite have one yet. She was too stunned. Only an hour ago she had been checking IDs at the club and thinking about fall semester and now here she was with the woman who had been filling nearly every lucid thought she'd had in weeks. She counted to twenty, silently in her head, and still there was nothing. Eons passed, the world turned and still…nothing. She watched Dusty turn toward the fireplace, wiping tears from her eyes.

"If you can't—I mean, if you can't love me back—that's okay too. I hurt you and I know that. I hurt you over and over, and all you did in return was save me."

She turned back around, searching Morgan's face. "Do you know what I saw when I got back to the lodge? An enormous cedar had crashed through that big picture window in my cabin. If I hadn't been hiking with you, I could have been hurt badly. You saved me when I froze when the landslide hit, you saved me by helping me talk about what had happened to me, you saved me when—" She stopped to catch her breath. "You saved me when I was on the verge of a panic attack in the club the night we met. You've saved me over and over."

Morgan remained silent as she tried to take in all that Dusty had been saying. She studied her face. She looked different now, more at peace. The opposite of the scared and haunted look she had worn not that long ago. Granted she still had work to do, but the words that she was saying and the way she was standing spoke volumes at how far she had come and how much she had worked to get herself back to Idaho.

She watched as tears fell from Dusty's eyes and trickled down her cheeks, as she wiped them from her face and took a deep breath, steadying herself.

"Anyway, that is all I wanted to tell you and that is why I am here." She held her hands open at her sides. "I can give you a ride back now if you want. I only wanted to show you my new place and…"

Morgan stood up. She took Dusty's hands into hers and placed a kiss in each palm. Looking up to meet her eyes, she wrapped Dusty's arms around her waist, leaned into her and brushed her lips against hers, letting the kiss linger before pressing her forehead to Dusty's.

"I am sorry it took me so long to figure everything out, Morgan. It wasn't just sex to me when we first made love. I wanted it to be, but when I looked into your eyes, it was so much more. You meant so much more."

Dusty ran her hands up Morgan's back and pulled her tight against her body. "I'm sorry I didn't wait for you at the lodge and that I ran again. I was scared. Scared that you'd hurt me. Scared that I'd hurt you. And I did, body and soul. It was easy to conclude that you'd be better off without me."

"You're wrong, Dusty. I wasn't better off without you. I was worse off, worse than I have ever been. You were in me, in every part of me. I fell in love with you—your mind, your heart, your ability to inspire others with your words."

Morgan pulled away. "I need to apologize to you too."

"What are you talking about?"

"I took advantage of you, the night you told me about Andrea. You shared your story with me; you poured your whole life out to me. And I woke up, early, before you did. I was holding you and instead of letting you go I held you even tighter. I knew you would be embarrassed, but I did it anyway. I couldn't let go and I drove you from the cabin that day. I should have woken you up."

"No, no, you didn't," said Dusty, finally kissing Morgan on the lips. "It wasn't anything that you did. I was scared about being in Idaho and what I was feeling for you. It was all too much at once." She gave Morgan a crooked smile. "I am kind of stunted that way."

"No. No, you are not. I know how difficult it was for you to be here," Morgan said. "I never forgot how wonderful you felt inside me, Dusty." She found Dusty's hand and intertwined their fingers.

"Morgan," Dusty whispered, "I never forgot either. It is all I thought about after I left your arms from making love to you the night we met—the night you found me." She lifted Morgan's hand to her lips, placing kisses on each of her fingers. "Will you please let me try again to love you? Will you let me try to show you how I feel today, tomorrow and the next day?"

"Yes," Morgan said as she pressed up against Dusty, looking into her eyes. Morgan's heart beat wildly in her chest as she leaned in for another kiss, meeting Dusty's lips. Their tongues teased each other. They ran their hands through each other's hair and down each other's backs, pressing into each other, their hold on each other growing tighter still.

"I was a really self-destructive person before I met you," said Dusty.

"I know you were," Morgan said into Dusty's lips.

"And I can take it slow. I'm fine with just talking and holding you, just being with you. That is all I want," Dusty whispered. "I want to know everything about you."

"Let me make love with you tonight, please," said Morgan, smiling.

CHAPTER THIRTY-EIGHT

Dusty took Morgan's hand and led her down the hallway to her bedroom. There wasn't much in there, save a bed made up in crisp white sheets, a small table with a Tiffany lamp atop it and Dusty's laptop and boxes full of belongings.

"Sit," Dusty said, leaning in for a kiss as she turned on the little lamp, bathing the room in a soft prismatic glow. She paused for a moment, looking at the beautiful woman sitting on her bed waiting for her.

Dusty got up onto the bed, knelt behind Morgan, and removed the tie from her golden hair, reveling in the way it felt in her hands.

"Morgan, did you know that every moment at the cabin was torture for me?" She continued to place gentle kisses on Morgan's neck, lingering at the places where she noticed her breathing increasing and her body tensing. "There wasn't a moment that passed where I didn't want you in my arms," she said as Morgan turned to meet her lips, gently licking them. The heat of her kisses caused a peace to settle within her.

"Kissing you, touching you, loving you were the only things I thought about too," Morgan said. Tears trailed down her cheek.

"Sweetheart, what's wrong?"

"Nothing. Absolutely nothing. I missed you. And now that you're here it's like a dream, and I don't ever want to wake up."

She smiled. "I missed you too, so much," she said with tears to match. "Thank you for chasing me down with my coat that night. Thank you for finding me."

"You found me, sweet girl. We found each other."

Dusty wrapped her arms around her, holding her tight. She felt Morgan place her hands over her own, ensuring that she would never let go. Dusty held her like that for a while, whispering things into her ear, things that made her smile, told her she was loved.

Dusty resumed placing kisses on Morgan's neck, her hands inching her way toward Morgan's breasts. She caressed them through her thin tube top and, as she pulled it down, watched Morgan's nipples instantly tighten.

"You take my breath away every time you touch me." Morgan squirmed in her arms. "Let me touch you."

"Not yet," Dusty said against her neck.

Morgan moaned as Dusty took her nipples and worked them into tight little peaks. She pulled her top the rest of the way off, taking her time, committing to memory the feel of her skin, the whispers that she heard in response.

"You feel so much better than I remember," she said, unbuttoning Morgan's jean cutoffs and zipping them open, causing Morgan to moan and lean back onto her body.

"Watch me love you, please?" The only response was a whimper into her neck. "Watch me," she said, placing a kiss on the side of her head.

* * *

With difficulty, Morgan opened her eyes to watch Dusty move her hand into her shorts and finger her aching center through her panties. "Touch me," she pleaded. "Please. I need to feel you."

Dusty did as she was told, tugging at Morgan's cutoffs and rolling down her panties. Morgan shimmied out of them and let Dusty pull her back between her legs and gently onto her stomach.

"Are you sure you are okay?" Dusty asked, as she opened Morgan's legs with her knee.

"Oh my God, yes," she whispered, watching Dusty spread her open and run her fingers through her length, the connection stoking her white-hot.

"I don't want to be rough with you, not this time."

"You can have me however you want."

Dusty added her thumb, brushing her sensitive center with each slow stroke into her. She needed to be taken tonight. She wanted to give herself utterly and completely to Dusty, wanted to give that to her. She was going to come soon. But Dusty continued to hold her at the edge.

"Always so wet for me," she whispered into Morgan's ear.

Dusty slid through Morgan's swollen center, causing her to rise and tremble. "Please, inside me," Morgan moaned, grabbing Dusty's hand.

Dusty entered her slowly. She slid one finger inside her before pulling out to add a second.

Morgan rewarded the action with a soft moan into her ear, a moan of longing fulfilled. "Fuck, you make me feel so good." She gripped Dusty's thigh to brace herself and, as much as she wanted to dance on the edge, she gave herself over and set herself free. Her cries were that of a pain soothed with love, the release that she had craved since the night she had fallen. Dusty's hold on her was ever tight. Her fingers, still inside and in sync with her desire, refused to let her go.

* * *

Dusty closed her eyes, relishing the feeling of being inside her lover. Finally, she slowly slid out, feeling Morgan tremble as she withdrew.

"You taste so wonderful," she said, realizing that Morgan was watching as she licked her essence off her fingers. She took her time, greedily licking Morgan's arousal off each finger. "So sweet. I can't get enough of you."

When she tried to take Morgan again, though, she was met with resistance. Overpowered. Pushed to her back and rewarded by Morgan with kisses that were ravenous and deep—as if she was searching for precious treasure. She smoothed Morgan's hair from her face and looked deep into her eyes. She pressed her forehead against hers. "I love you," she whispered into Morgan's lips.

"I love you," she replied, resuming her kisses. Morgan trusted her. Her kisses told her so. They said that she was beautiful, worthy, and worth it.

When Morgan touched her, she was ready. She melted into the contact, feeling Morgan's fingers sliding easily up her length and down.

"Come for me."

"Only for you," she whispered. And then "Yes!"—said over and over and over as she let Morgan reach deep inside her, surrendering to the woman who filled her heart and soul as nobody else ever had or would. She vowed to be as gentle and careful with Morgan's heart, to hold it as if it were made of delicate spun crystal, for the rest of their lives together.

Morgan moved her hands to Dusty's legs and spread her legs further apart with the palms of her hands. She lifted them up and bent them at the knee, opening her even more to her, and continued to lick her. "So sweet." She moved in and out of Dusty like waves on a beach, totally in sync with Dusty's breathing, her eyes locked onto Dusty's. Dusty wanted to close her eyes, to give herself over, but she held on to Morgan's gaze until she was on the very edge. Until Morgan pushed her over, let her fall and then caught her midflight and lifted her up, making her come in a blinding explosion.

"Morgan…" Dusty reached down for her, pulling her up her body, and kissed Morgan's eyelids, then her lips. She held Morgan close and tight. "I'll never let you go ever again. Never."

"I don't want you to," Morgan said. Dusty stroked her hair, getting ready to take her yet again to heights unknown. Getting ready to wake up in the morning with Morgan sleeping next to her, not simply because she was in Dusty's home, but because Dusty had come home.

Bella Books, Inc.

Women. Books. Even Better Together.

P.O. Box 10543
Tallahassee, FL 32302

Phone: 800-729-4992
www.bellabooks.com